PROJECTS WINDOWS®
FOR BEGINNERS

Program Manager

Recorder

Object Packager

Cardfile

Control Panel

Philippa Wingate

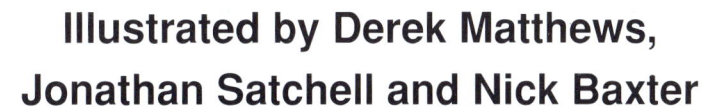

Illustrated by Derek Matthews, Jonathan Satchell and Nick Baxter

File Manager

Paintbrush

Sound Recorder

Write

Character Map

Designed by Paul Greenleaf and Neil Francis
Russell Punter, Non Figg and Rachel Wells

Technical Consultant: Richard Payne

Edited by Anthony Marks and Jane Chisholm

Contents

- 3   What is this book about?
- 4   Windows basics
- 6   Changing your Windows display
- 8   Customizing your desktop
- 10   Super screen savers
- 12   Using Write
- 14   More news on using Write  
- 16   Using Paintbrush
- 18   Design your own wallpaper
- 20   Greetings and invitations
- 22   The personal touch
- 24   Outlines and stencils
- 26   All change
- 28   Mouse mats
- 30   Stickers and scenes
- 32   A picture address book
- 34   Character maps and codes
- 36   Invent your own quiz game  
- 38   Finding a hidden message
- 40   Interactive storytime
- 42   Macro magic
- 44   Cartoon fun
- 46   Windows 95
- 48   Index

What is this book about?

Windows® is a piece of computer software made by a company called Microsoft®. It is used on millions of personal computers around the world.

When you buy Windows, it contains a set of applications. These include Control Panel, Write, Paintbrush, Cardfile, Character Map, Recorder and Object Packager. This book shows how you can use these applications to tackle a variety of projects.

Versions and updates

Experts at Microsoft are constantly trying to find ways of improving the way in which Windows works. From time to time, they produce a new version of the software which includes all their recent improvements.

Each version is given a number, the higher the number, the more up-to-date the version. The projects in this book are demonstrated using version 3.1 of Windows. You'll still be able to do them if you have version 3.11 or Windows® for Workgroups 3.1 and 3.11.

Some of the different versions of Windows available

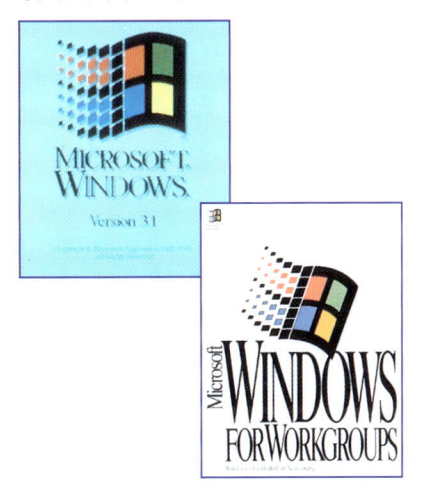

Windows 95

There is a version of Windows called Windows® 95 which is quite different from Windows 3.1. You can find out about some of the main differences on pages 46 and 47.

Using this book

To use this book it is helpful to have a basic knowledge of how to use the applications included in Windows. Brief explanations of how to operate the main applications, however, are included in the book.

Each project is described with clear, step-by-step instructions. The projects get more complicated towards the end of the book, so it's a good idea to work your way through from beginning to end.

Essential equipment

To complete many of the projects in this book all you need is a computer and Windows software. The book assumes that your Windows software has been installed in a "typical" way. The project instructions are written for a right-handed mouse user.

To print pictures and letters, you will need a printer. If you don't have a colour printer, make sure you have pens or paints to decorate your print-outs.

If you want to send project files to your friends, you'll need floppy disks to transfer the files.

This is the only equipment you'll need to tackle most of the projects in this book.

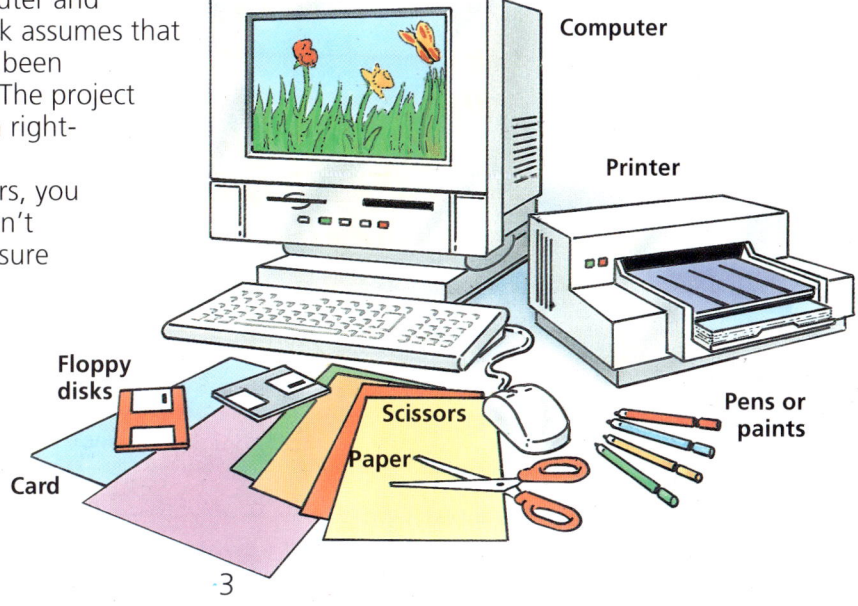

Windows basics

On these two pages you can find out about the different parts of a Windows display. There are some basic tips about how to control a window and how to open and close an application. There is also some advice on saving and storing any files you create.

Windows, icons and your desktop

A basic Windows display is made up of windows, icons and a background layer called the desktop. The picture below shows you some of the main parts of a Windows display and tells you their names.

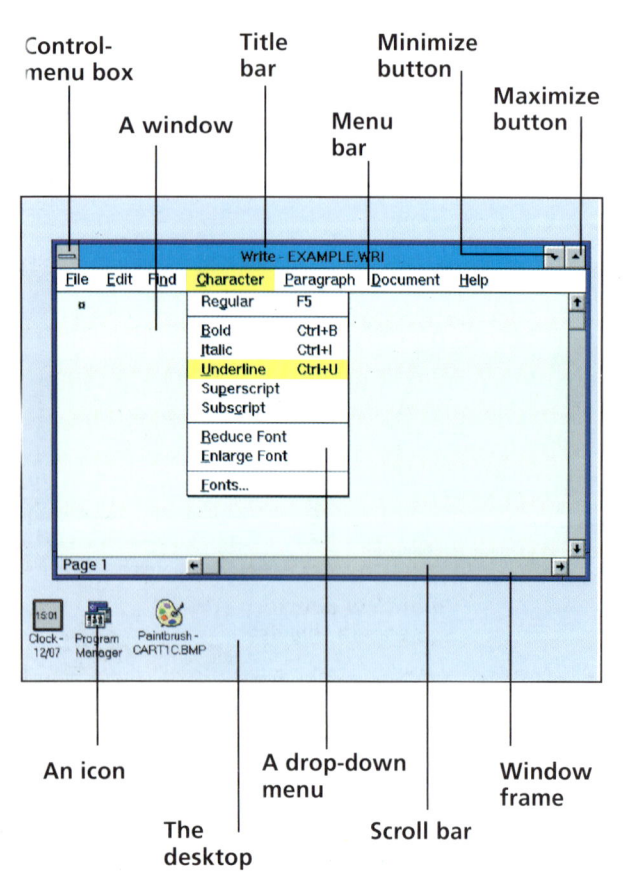

Control-menu box
Title bar
Minimize button
Maximize button
A window
Menu bar
An icon
The desktop
A drop-down menu
Scroll bar
Window frame

Program Manager

When you first start up Windows 3.1, a window called Program Manager appears on your screen. If it appears as an icon at the bottom of your screen, double-click on it to open the window.

This is the Program Manager icon.

All the instructions for the projects in this book start from Program Manager. For these instructions to work properly, you need to open Program Manager's *Options* menu and click on *Minimize on Use*, so that a tick appears beside it, as in the picture below.

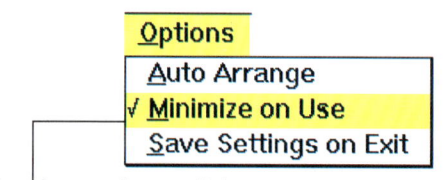

Options
Auto Arrange
√ Minimize on Use
Save Settings on Exit

To select an item, click on it in the menu.

Opening an application

All the applications on your computer are grouped together in program groups inside the Program Manager window.

This is a program group icon.

Games

To open a program group, double-click on its icon. A new window will open inside Program Manager. It will contain the icons of all the applications in that particular group.

Each standard Windows application has a different icon. An icon usually gives you an idea of what its application is used for. For example, this icon is for File Manager, which is an application used to organize the files on your computer. The icon looks like a filing cabinet.

To open an application, simply double-click your pointer on its icon.

4

Re-sizing a window

When an application opens, a window appears on your screen containing the work-space in which you use the application. You can change the shape of the window by clicking on its frame and dragging it into the shape you want.

To make a window fill your whole screen, click on its Maximize button.

This window is being re-sized to a smaller size.

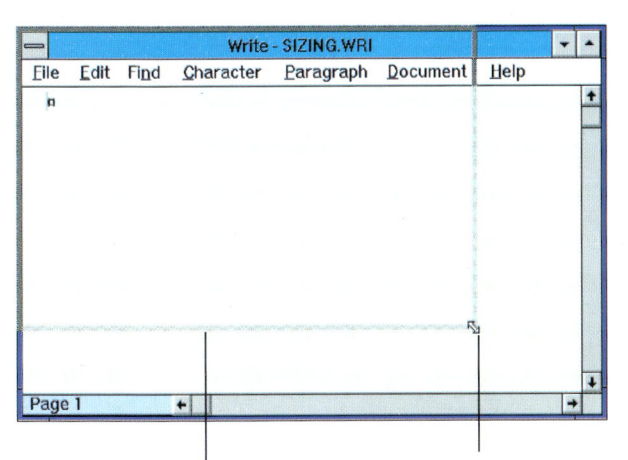

This outline shows you the new size of the window.

With this re-sizing pointer, drag the window into the shape you want.

Minimizing applications

You can have several applications running on your computer at once. To make sure that you have enough space on your desktop to use an application properly, it's a good idea to minimize the windows of other applications. To do this, click on their Minimize buttons. They will appear as icons at the bottom of your screen. They are still running, and you can "restore" them to their former size, by double-clicking on their icons.

Closing an application

If you have finished using an application and want to close it down completely, select *Exit* in the application's *File* menu. Another, quicker way of closing an application is to double-click in its control-menu box.

Directories

All the files stored on a computer's hard disk are grouped together in directories. Make a new directory for the files you will create while doing the projects in this book. This will keep them separate from all the other information on your computer.

Creating a new directory

To create a "projects" directory, open the File Manager application by double-clicking on its icon in Program Manager. Inside its window there will be one or more windows. Close all but one of these windows. Select *Select Drive* in the *Disk* menu and in the dialog box highlight the hard disk drive (usually the C drive). The window will now display the directories on the hard disk.

Click on the folder symbol at the top of the list which has C:\ written next to it (see below). Select *Create Directory...* in the *File* menu. A Create Directory dialog box will appear. In the *Name* box, type PROJECTS and click OK. A projects directory will appear in the list. Find out how to put files into this directory on page 12.

File Manager's window with a projects directory

The C:\ folder symbol

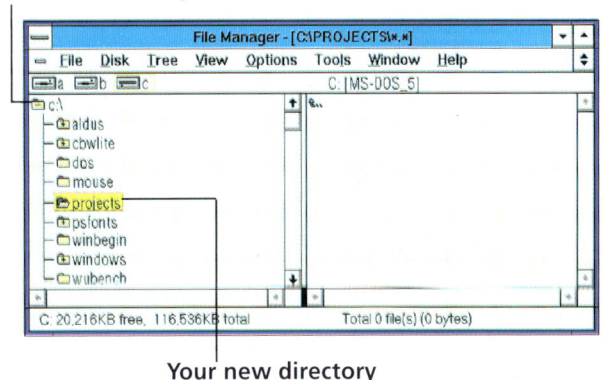

Your new directory appears in this list.

Take care

Make sure that you don't delete or change any files already stored on the hard disk of the computer you are using.

Changing your Windows display

If you have a colour monitor, the desktop, windows and icons which make up a Windows display will be multicoloured. If you have a black and white monitor, the display will be black, white and shades of grey. You can change the appearance of your display using the programs found in the Control Panel application.

Control Panel

Control Panel is usually found in the program group called Main. Open it by double-clicking on its icon in the Program Manager window.

This is the Control Panel icon.

Things to avoid

When using Control Panel avoid the following programs: Network, Ports, Keyboard, International, 386 Enhanced, Drivers. They won't alter the appearance of your display, and changing them could cause problems with your computer hardware.

Avoid these icons in Control Panel.

Printers   International   Ports

Keyboard   386 Enhanced   Drivers

Changing colour schemes

To change the colour schemes of the windows and desktop that make up your Windows display, double-click on the Color icon in the Control Panel window.

This is the Color icon.

In the Color window that appears, open the *Color Schemes* list. It contains a selection of colour combinations, with names like Arizona, Tweed or Hotdog Stand. Try one out by highlighting its name in the list. The sample display below the list will change to show you what your chosen colour scheme looks like.

The sample Windows display in this Color window is showing a scheme called Patchwork.

The sample Windows display

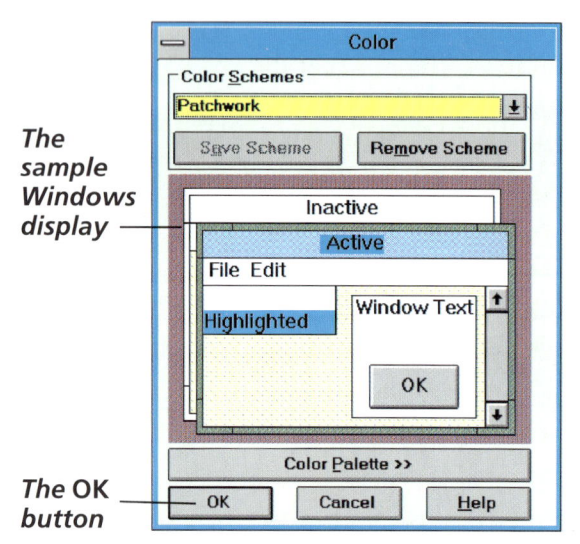

The OK button

When you have found a scheme you like, click the *OK* button. The Color window will close and the display will show your new colours.

Choosing your own colours

If you don't like any of the existing Windows colour schemes, you can create your own. In the Color window, click on the *Color Palette>>* button. The window will extend to show a palette of colours.

The Basic Colors palette

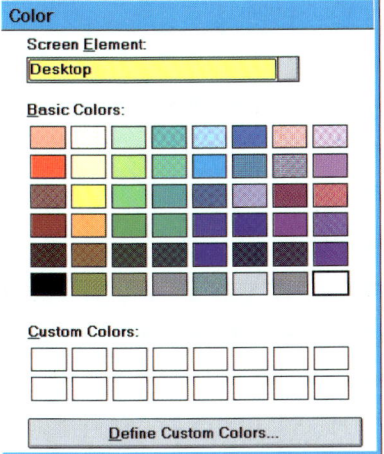

Click on any element of the sample Windows display, such as the "Active Title Bar" or the "Menu Bar". The name of the element you have selected will appear in the *Screen Element* box. Now choose a new colour for this element by clicking on any of the coloured squares in the *Basic Colors* palette.

Mixing colours

Like an artist, you can mix up your own selection of dazzling new colours.

To do this, click on an empty square in the *Custom Colors* section. Click the *Define Custom Colors...* button. A dialog box appears containing a multicoloured square. Select the colour in any part of the square by clicking on it. To add this colour to your palette, click the *Add Color* button. To close the Custom Color Selector box, click the *Close* button.

The Custom Color Selector box

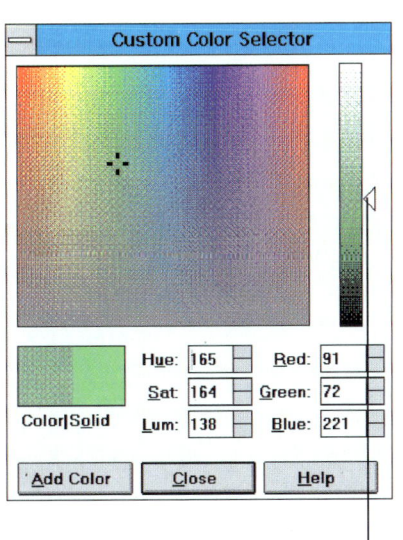

Drag this pointer up and down to change the brightness of your new colour.

Saving a scheme

When you have designed a colour scheme that you are happy with, you need to save it. In the Color window, click the *Save Scheme* button. A dialog box appears. Type in a name for your scheme, such as Blue Boomerang or Peachy Pig Pink and click *OK*.

Displaying a scheme

To display your colours on screen, close the Color window by clicking the *OK* button at the bottom left-hand corner of the window. Your personal colour scheme will automatically appear on the screen.

Black and white

If you have a black and white monitor you can still change the appearance of your display. There are different shades and textures to choose from in the *Color Palette* dialog box.

Some of the schemes in the *Color Schemes* list begin with the letters LCD. These combinations are specially designed for use on monochrome monitors and laptop computers. Try some of them out using the technique described above.

Customizing your desktop

There are other ways in which you can change the Windows display. You can change the pattern that decorates the desktop using the Control Panel application.

How to see your desktop

To make sure that you can see the desktop of your Windows display, double-click on the Control Panel icon in Program Manager.

This is the Desktop icon. Double-click on it and the Desktop window will appear. In this window there is a section called Wallpaper. Open up the *File* list and highlight *(None)*.

The Wallpaper section of the Desktop window

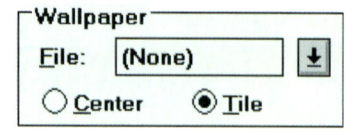

When you click *OK* in the top right-hand corner of the Desktop window, you will be able to see the desktop at the back of your screen.

Colouring your desktop

To change the colour of your desktop, use the Color program in Control Panel. You can read about how to change the colour elements of your display on page 6 and 7. Select the desktop on the sample Windows display and assign it a new colour in the *Colour Palette*.

Patterns on your desktop

The patterns which you can choose to decorate your desktop are made up of small patterns repeated hundreds of times to fill your screen.

In the section of the Desktop window called Pattern, open the *Name* list. This shows you all the desktop patterns provided by Windows.

The Pattern section of the Desktop window

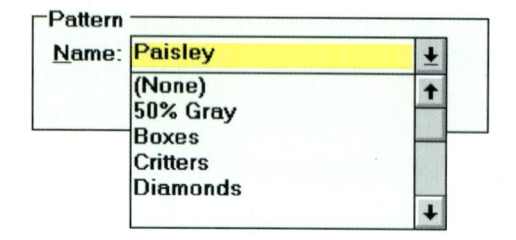

To try out one of the patterns, such as Boxes or Scottie, highlight its name in the *File* list. Click the *OK* button and your desktop background will immediately change.

Two of Window's desktop patterns.

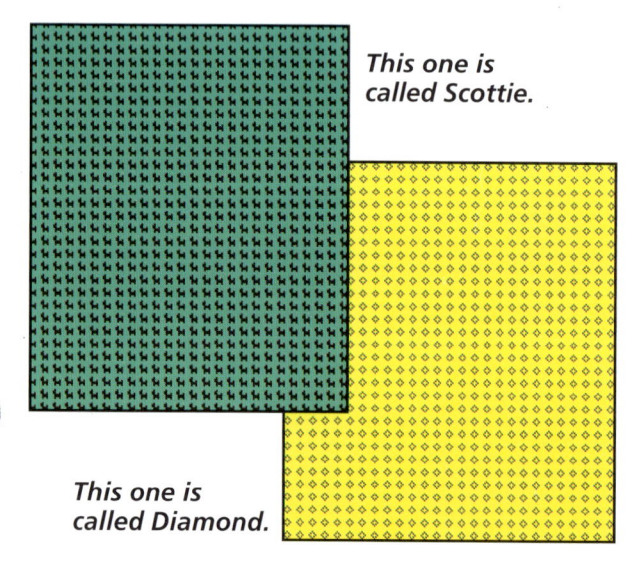

This one is called Scottie.

This one is called Diamond.

8

How to design your own desktop pattern

If you don't like any of the existing desktop patterns provided by Windows, you can design your own. In the Desktop window, open the *Name* list in the Pattern section and select *(None)*. Click the *Edit Pattern...* button and a dialog box will open.

In the Edit Pattern dialog box there are two empty boxes. The larger one is covered with lots of invisible squares. When you click anywhere in this square with your pointer, a small black square will appear. If you click on it again, the small black square will disappear.

This is the Edit Pattern dialog box.

The name of your pattern.

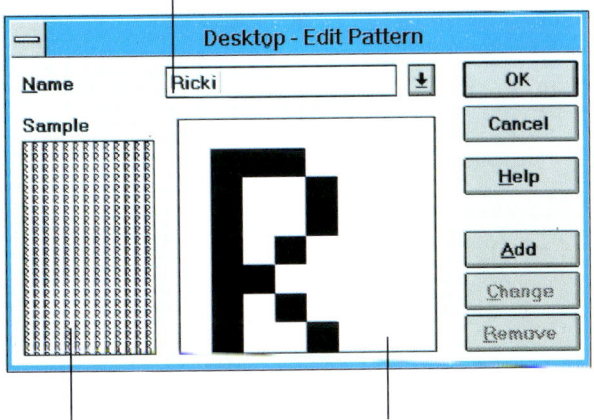

This is the Sample box which shows you what your pattern will look like.

This is the box in which you draw your pattern.

Using this technique create new shapes and patterns by adding black boxes. As you change the pattern, you can see the effect it will have on your desktop in the box called Sample.

Changing existing patterns

You can also change some of the existing desktop patterns. Select one of them and then click on *Edit Pattern...* Using your pointer, alter the pattern of the black squares.

A selection of the patterns you can create.

You can use a letter.

The box in which the pattern is drawn.

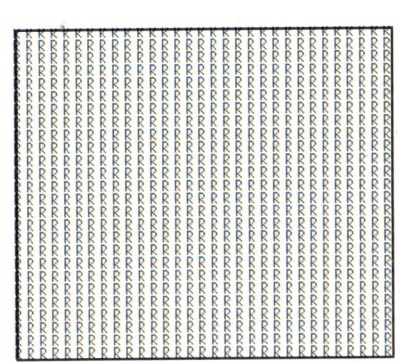

Stripes look good.

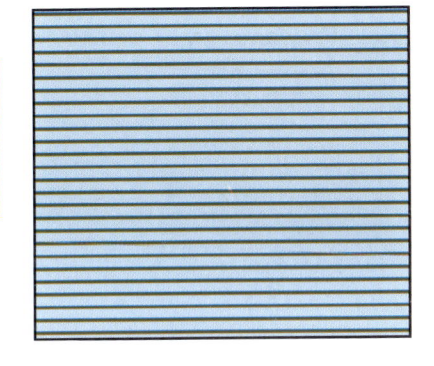

Naming your pattern

When you have created a pattern that you like and want to keep, give it a name in the *Name* box, such as Stripes or Rings. Then click the *Add* button.

To close the Desktop - Edit Pattern dialog box, click the *OK* button. When you do this, you will immediately see your new pattern covering the desktop.

9

Super screen savers

If you leave the same image displayed on your screen for a long time, it becomes permanently imprinted on the screen glass. This is called screen burn. To avoid it, you can use a program called screen saver, which replaces the image with a moving picture after a certain amount of time. Windows provides a selection of different moving images that you can alter and personalize.

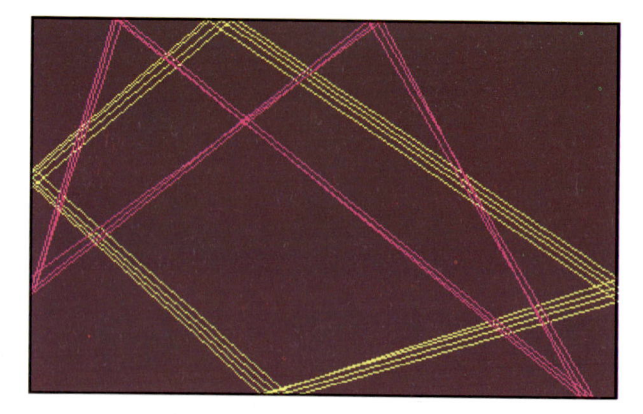

This screen saver is called Mystify.

Turning on a screen saver

To choose a Windows screen saver, double-click on the Control Panel icon in Program Manager. In the Control Panel window, double-click on the Desktop icon. There is a section of the Desktop window called Screen Saver. Open the *Name* list and you will find a list of screen savers available on your computer.

This is the Screen Saver dialog box

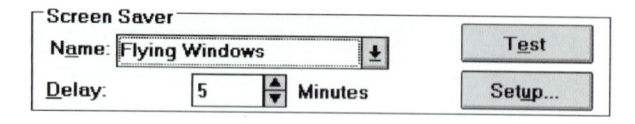

Try out one of them, say Flying Windows, by highlighting its name and then clicking on the *Test* button. If you use the Flying Windows screen saver, your screen will change to show lots of Windows logos rushing towards you.

A screen showing Flying Windows screen saver

Stopping a screen saver

Screen savers are designed to disappear from the screen the moment you move your mouse or press any of the keys on the keyboard. Stop the test demonstration of a screen saver by doing either of these things.

Setting a delay time

You can instruct your computer to start a screen saver automatically when you leave it unused for a certain amount of time. By clicking on the upward or the downward arrows on the right-hand side of the *Delay* box, you can alter the number of minutes your computer is idle before the screen saver is activated.

Making changes

You can alter the colours and speed of some of the Windows screen savers. To do this, highlight the screen saver you want to alter in the *Name* list. Click the *Setup...* button and a Setup dialog box will appear.

This is the Mystify Setup dialog box.

Make sure *Active* is selected.

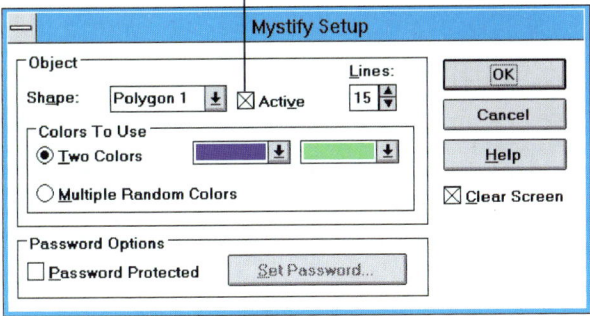

With the Mystify screen saver, for example, you can change the shape, colour and the number of lines which make up the shapes, called polygons, that appear on your screen.

You can decide whether the screen goes black when the screen saver starts or whether the polygons gradually black out the screen. When you have selected your preferences, click *OK*.

Personal messages

If you choose to use the Marquee screen saver, you can write a message that will travel across your screen. Select a colour for the letters and the background. Type in your message in the *Text* box section. You can also choose the speed at which the words will travel. Finally, click *OK*.

This is the Marquee Setup dialog box.

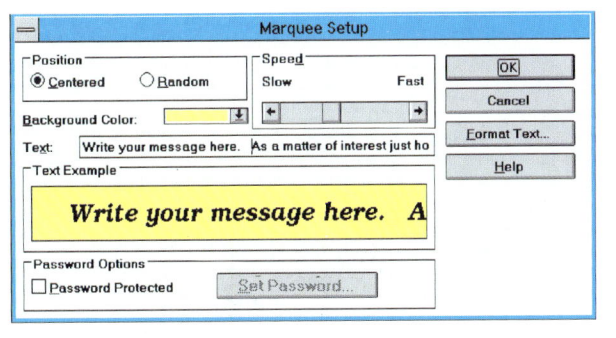

Passwords

In the Setup boxes of each screen saver you are given the option of putting a password on your screen saver. This means that when the screen saver comes on it will remain "locked" on the screen until you type in a special password.

It's not a good idea to put a password on your screen saver. You might forget the password and nobody would be able to use the computer until a computer expert unlocked the screen saver.

Click your pointer in the box beside *Password Protected* in the *Password Options* section until there is no cross in the box.

This is the Password Options section.

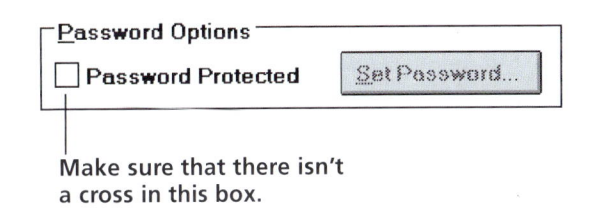

Make sure that there isn't a cross in this box.

Ready to go

When you have selected the screen saver you want, click the *OK* button and close the Control Panel window by double-clicking in its control-menu box.

Your screen saver is now activated. Whenever you leave your computer for the period of time you have specified, the screen saver will appear.

11

Using Write

Write is an application that allows you to type in text and organize it into a document. You will use it in many of the projects in this book. To open Write, double-click on its icon in Program Manager.

This is the Write icon.

A window opens containing a blank page. A flashing cursor in the left-hand corner indicates where your text appears when you start typing.

This is a Write window.

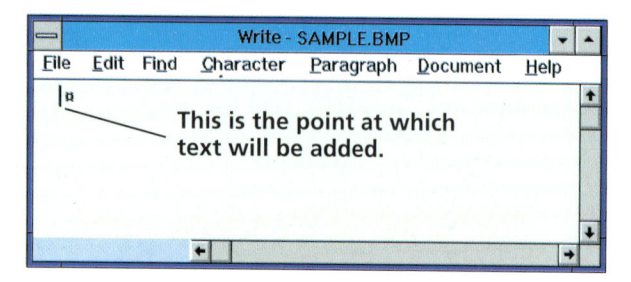

Type a filename in the *File Name* box. It can have up to eight letters or numbers. All Write files have the extension .WRI. So select *.WRI in the *Save File as Type* box. In the *Drives* list highlight the disk drive which contains the disk you want to save your file on.

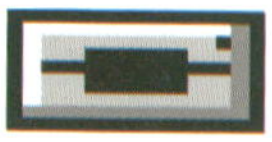

Floppy disk drives have icons like this beside them.

The hard disk drive (usually the C drive) has an icon like this.

To put your file into your projects directory (see page 5), double-click on the C:\ folder at the top of the *Directories* list. In the list that appears, double-click on the projects directory and then click *OK*.

This method of saving a file is similar to the technique you will use to save and store any file created in a Windows application.

Saving a Write file

When you have typed in some text, such as a letter or a story, you should save your Write document. Open the *File* menu and select *Save As...* The following dialog box will appear.

A Save As dialog box

Type in the name of your file here.

Select the directory in which you want to store your file.

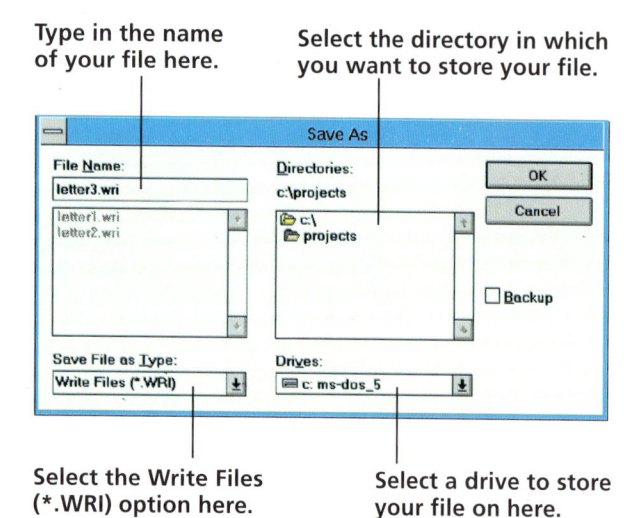

Select the Write Files (*.WRI) option here.

Select a drive to store your file on here.

Printing out a Write file

To print out a Write file, you need to have a printer installed and connected to your computer. Make sure that it is switched on and "on line", which means that it is ready to receive data from your computer.

Select *Open...* in Write's *File* menu. In the dialog box highlight the name of the file you want to print. Click *OK* and the document will appear in Write's window.

Select *Print Setup...* in the *File* menu. Check that the type of printer you are using is specified in the Printer section. In the Paper section, check that the size of the paper you are using is highlighted. Then click *OK*.

Select *Print...* in Write's *File* menu. If your document has more than one page, specify which pages you want to print. Enter the number of copies of your document you want. Finally, click *OK* to begin printing.

Letterheads

You don't have to type your name and address at the top of every letter you send. You can store this information in a Write document called a letterhead.

Creating a letterhead

Open a copy of Write and type in the information you want in your letterhead. This usually includes your name, address, telephone and fax number, but you may want to include other information too.

A selection of printed letterheads and notepaper

Arranging text

You can arrange your letterhead information wherever you like on the page. To arrange any text, you must highlight it first. To do this, click your cursor at the beginning of the block of text you want to arrange and drag it to the end. Release the mouse button, and your text will appear highlighted, like **this**.

Highlight your letterhead information in this way, and in the *Paragraph* menu select *Left*, *Right* or *Centered*, depending on where you want your text to appear on the page.

Saving your letterhead

When you are ready, select *Save As...* in Write's *File* menu. Give your file a name (letrhead.wri, for example). Place it in your projects directory and save it.

To write a letter, open letrhead.wri and type in your message underneath the letterhead information. Select *Save As...* in the *File* menu and give your letter a new filename (such as letter.wri). This will ensure that your letterhead file remains unaltered.

Brighter letters

When you print out a letter, you can add colour and patterns to it with pens or paints. In the picture below, the letterheads have been printed on coloured paper. Bright patterns and borders have been added. You can make your own notepaper by printing your letterhead file onto several sheets of paper and adding a handwritten note.

More news on using Write

You can use Write to create leaflets or newsletters. By exploring the different styles and shapes of text available and varying the size and position of your text, you can produce professional-looking documents.

Using different text styles

One way of making text easier to read and understand is to use different text styles to emphasize important information. Write's *Character* menu provides a selection of text styles from which you can choose. Each one alters the appearance of text on the page, making it stand out from ordinary type. The different styles available are:

Bold, which makes text darker.

Italic, which makes text lean to the right.

Underline, which puts a line underneath text.

To use any of these styles, highlight the block of text you wish to alter (see page 13). Then select *Bold, Italic* or Underline in the *Character* menu.

A letter showing different text styles in Write

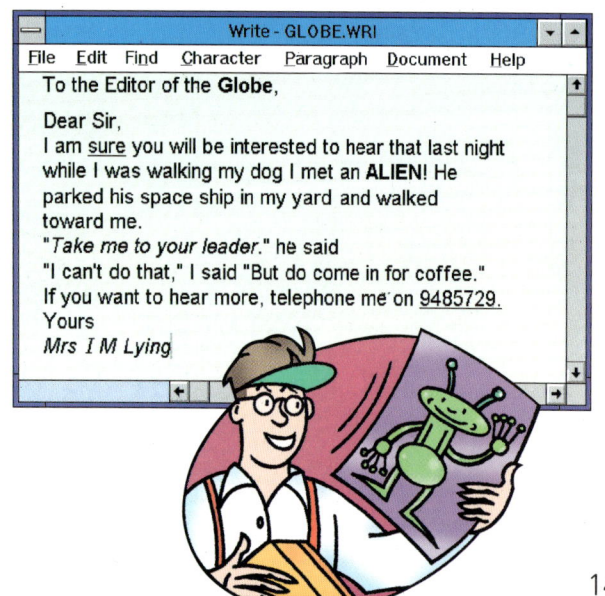

Fonts

A font is a set of letters, numbers or symbols which have a unique shape and appearance.

THIS IS A FONT CALLED "BOSANOVA".

This is a font called "Briquet".

Stored on a computer is a selection of fonts that you can use to produce a document. Some fonts are provided with Windows software, but you can also increase the range of fonts on your computer by buying extra software.

Trying out different fonts

Open Write and type in some text. Highlight the text you want to change to a different font. In the *Character* menu select *Fonts...* A Fonts dialog box opens like the one below.

A Fonts dialog box

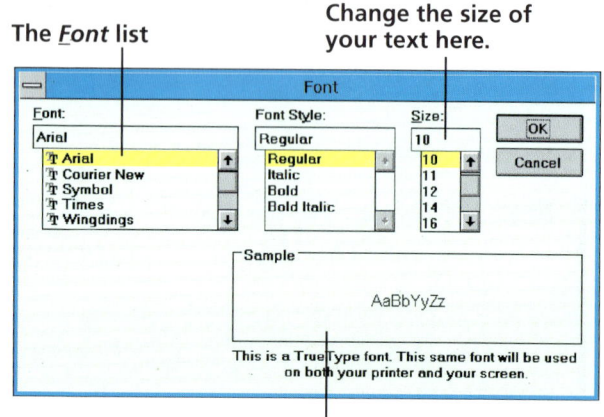

The *Font* list **Change the size of your text here.**

A sample of the selected font

If you select a font in the *Font* list, a sample of it appears in the Sample box. When you have found one you like, click *OK* and your text will appear in the new font.

You can also change the size of highlighted text by changing the number in the *Size* section of the Font dialog box. The higher the number, the larger your text.

This text is size 18.

This text is the same font, but size 12.

Making your own newsletter

Newspapers use a variety of different text styles and fonts. You may also have noticed that the text is usually arranged in narrow columns. You can use all these techniques to produce a newsletter like the one shown here.

A narrow column of text

To create a narrow column of text, select *Ruler On* in the *Document* menu. A ruler appears at the top of your page. At the left-hand end of the Ruler is a triangular marker. This indicates the left-hand edge of your text column.

At the right-hand end of the ruler is another marker marking the right-hand edge of your text column. Click your cursor on it and drag it toward the left-hand side of your page. Using the measurements on the Ruler, position this triangle at the column width you require.

Now, when you type in your news story, it will appear in a neat column.

A narrow column of text in Write

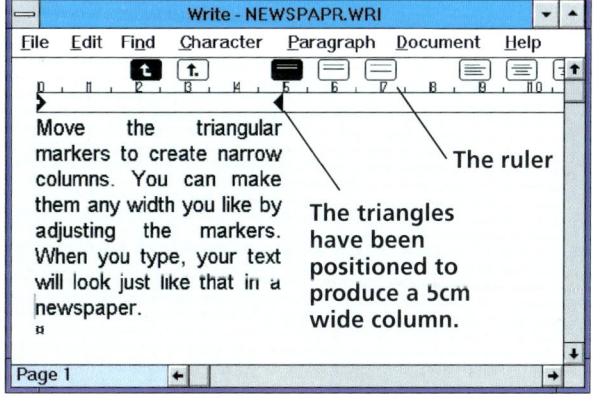

Move the triangular markers to create narrow columns. You can make them any width you like by adjusting the markers. When you type, your text will look just like that in a newspaper.

The ruler

The triangles have been positioned to produce a 5cm wide column.

Justified text

Many newspapers use justified text. This means that the words in each line have been spaced out to fill the width of the column. To make your text justified, highlight it and select *Justified* in the *Paragraph* menu.

To make your newsletter more colourful, you can use felt-tips or stick in photographs.

Finishing off

When you have printed out a selection of stories for your newsletter, paste them onto a large sheet of paper. Add lines to divide the columns of text and draw some pictures. When it is ready, photocopy and distribute your newsletter.

Using Paintbrush

This is the icon for Paintbrush, an application that enables you to create pictures. It is used in many of the projects in this book. A sample Paintbrush window is shown below.

A Paintbrush window

The Toolbox has 18 drawing tools that create different effects.

This is the canvas area where you draw your picture.

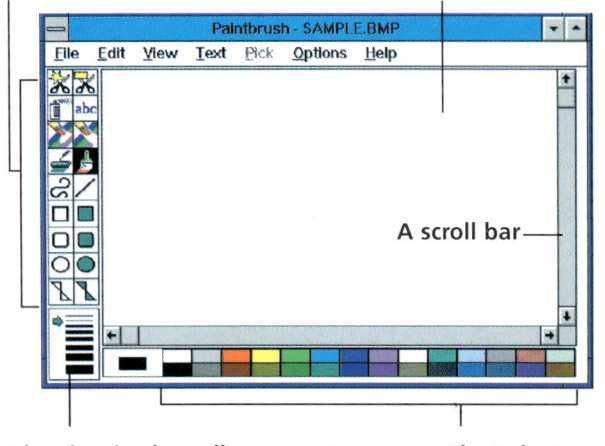

A scroll bar

The Linesize box allows you to select the width of your tools.

The Palette of colours

Sizing your canvas

To create a canvas of a particular size, select *Image Attributes...* in the *Options* menu. A dialog box appears like the one below:

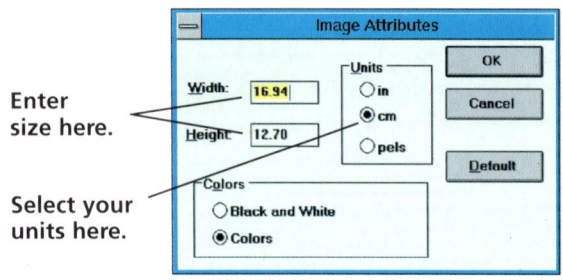

Enter size here.

Select your units here.

Type in the width and height of the canvas you require in the boxes. Make sure that centimetres is selected in the *Units* section. When you click *OK*, your canvas changes size.

If the canvas you are working on is too large to fit in Paintbrush's window, scroll bars will appear. By clicking on them, you can move around the whole canvas area.

Choosing new colours

There are two main types of colour in Paintbrush: the foreground colour and the background colour. The foreground colour is the one you use to draw things. The background colour is the colour of the canvas on which you are drawing.

To pick a foreground colour, click on a colour in the Palette with your left-hand mouse button. To select a background colour, click with your right-hand mouse button. The box at the left-hand end of the Palette shows the colours currently selected for the foreground and background.

Part of the Paintbrush Palette

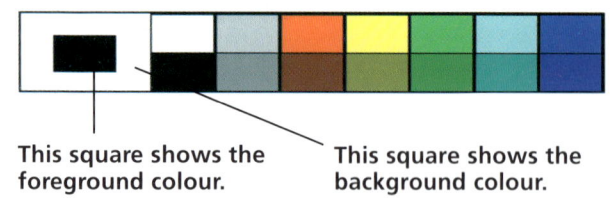

This square shows the foreground colour.

This square shows the background colour.

Creating a picture

You can use any of the tools in Paintbrush's Toolbox to draw a picture. To select a new tool, click on its icon in the panel. To paint with it, drag your cursor over the canvas area. The best way to find out how all the different tools work is to experiment with them. Some of the more complicated tools are explained in greater detail in the projects where you need to use them.

Erasing mistakes

You can correct any mistakes you make when drawing a Paintbrush picture. Highlight the Eraser tool and move it over the area you want to erase.

This is the Eraser tool icon.

Alternatively, select *Undo* in the *Edit* menu, to undo everything you have done since you chose a new tool or colour.

Saving a picture

To save a Paintbrush picture, select *Save As...* in the *File* menu. The dialog box below appears.

The Save As dialog box

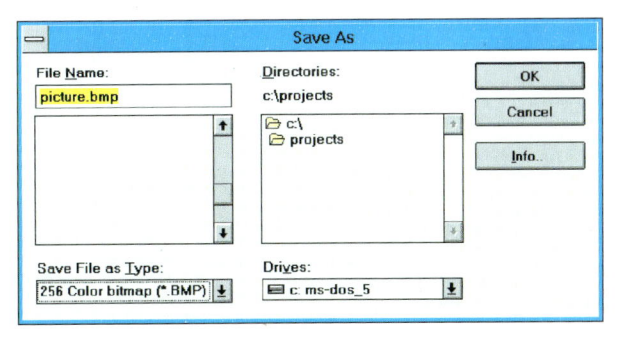

Give your picture a filename. Paintbrush filenames are always given the extension .BMP, so select *.BMP in the *Save File as Type* box. Place it in the projects directory and save it.

New pictures

When you want to start a new canvas, simply select *New* in the *File* menu. A new canvas will automatically appear. It will be exactly the same size as the one you used previously.

Printing out a picture

If you have a printer installed and connected to your computer and it is on line, you can print out a Paintbrush picture. To do this, select *Open...* in the *File* menu. Select the name of the file you want to print and click OK. Select *Print...* from the *File* menu. A Print dialog box appears, containing a selection of print options.

This is the Print dialog box.

For the best quality printing, select *Proof*.

In this section you can choose to print a small area of your picture, or all of it.

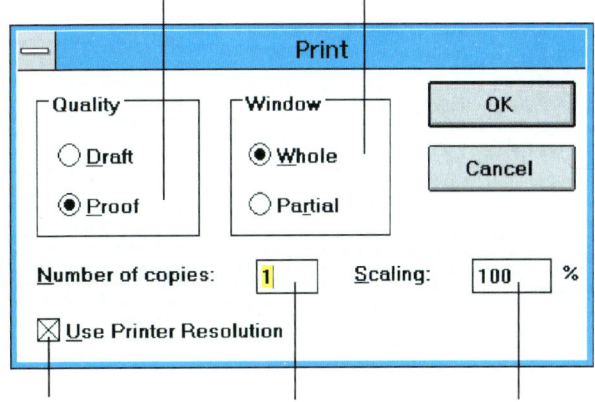

Make sure that *Use Printer Resolution* is selected here.

Choose the number of copies you require here.

Use the *Scaling* section to enlarge or reduce the size of your picture.

To make sure that your picture is printed as clearly as possible, select *Proof* in the *Quality* section. Make sure that *Whole* is selected in the *Window* section. This will ensure that all of your picture is printed, not just the area you can see in the Paintbrush window.

Type in the number of copies of your picture you want to print. Use the *Scaling* section to specify the size at which you want your picture to be printed out.

When you are ready, click the OK button to begin printing.

17

Design your own wallpaper

You can cover your desktop with a layer of patterns or pictures called wallpaper. Choose a wallpaper from the patterns Windows provides, or design your own.

These screens show two of the Windows wallpapers

This one is called leaves.bmp.

This one is called world.bmp.

Choosing a new wallpaper

To choose a wallpaper for your screen, double-click on the Control Panel icon in Program Manager. Then double-click on the Desktop icon. In the Desktop window there is a Wallpaper section.

To ensure that the wallpaper you are about to choose appears all over the back of your screen, click in the circle beside *Tile* until a dot appears.

The Wallpaper section

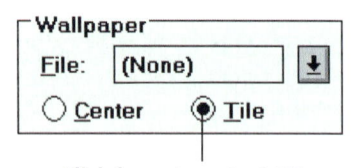

Click here to select *Tile*.

Now open the *File* list which contains the names of all the Windows wallpapers. They have names such as cars.bmp or zigzag.bmp. Try out one of them by highlighting it and clicking OK. The Desktop window will close and the new wallpaper will appear at the back of your screen.

Customizing

To alter a Windows wallpaper, open a copy of Paintbrush. Select *Open...* in the *File* menu.

In the dialog box that appears, select the windows directory in the *Directories* section. Then, in the File *Name* section, select the name of the wallpaper you want to alter. When you click OK, part of that wallpaper will appear on your canvas. You can add colours and patterns to it.

Color Eraser

A useful tool for customizing wallpaper is the Color Eraser. Select it by clicking on its icon in the Toolbox.

This is the Color Eraser icon.

The Color Eraser allows you to change the colours in a picture without altering the pattern. For example, if you don't like the blue areas of a wallpaper design, select that blue in the Palette with your left-hand mouse button. Select the colour you would like to replace it with, say red, with the right-hand mouse button. Then, hold down the left-hand button and, with your cursor, shade over the wallpaper design on your canvas.

Using Color Eraser

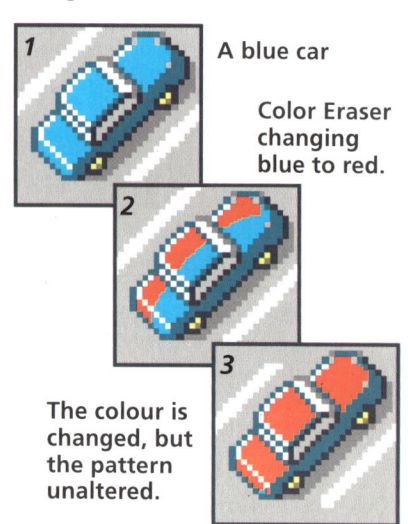

1. A blue car

Color Eraser changing blue to red.

2.

3. The colour is changed, but the pattern unaltered.

Make sure that the original wallpaper file remains unaltered by saving your new wallpaper file under a different filename.

Make your own wallpaper

You can design your own wallpaper using Paintbrush. A wallpaper appears on your desktop in tiles. The number of tiles that are needed to cover the desktop depends on the size of the canvas you use to create a wallpaper. If you draw on a small canvas (say, about 2cm by 2cm), it will be repeated many times to cover your desktop. If you choose a larger canvas (say, 6cm by 6cm), it will only be repeated a few times.

Open Paintbrush and select *Image Attributes...* in the *Options* menu. Enter the measurements of the canvas you require and click *OK*.

Two sample wallpaper designs

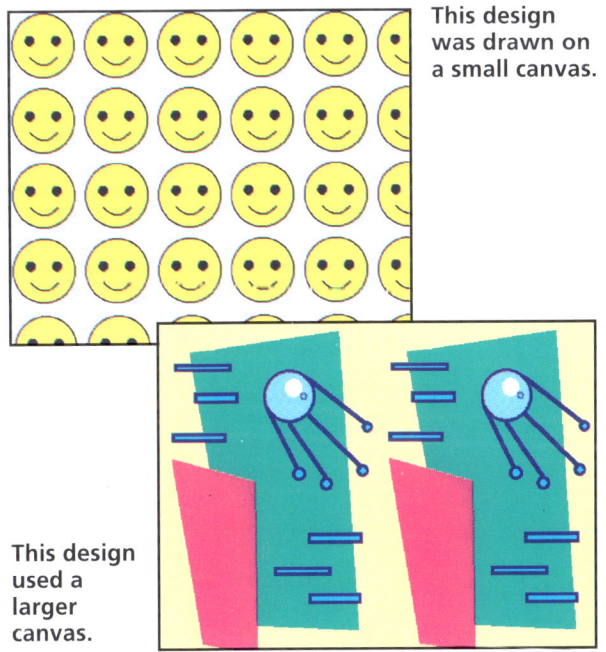

This design was drawn on a small canvas.

This design used a larger canvas.

Design a tile of wallpaper using any of the tools and colours Paintbrush offers. The Paintbrush window below shows a large tile of wallpaper.

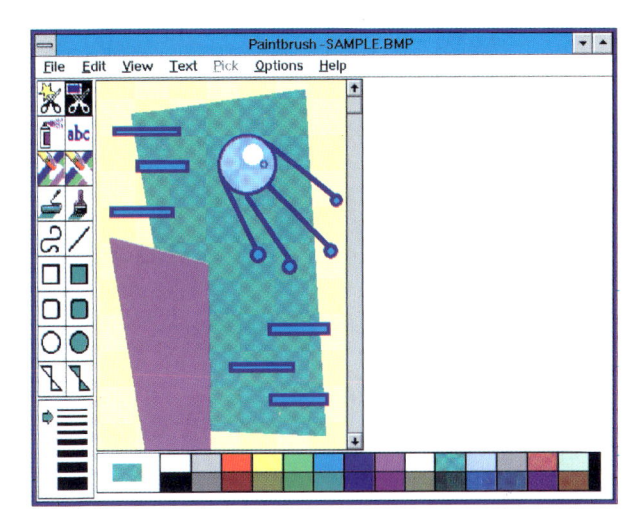

Naming wallpaper files

When you have finished your wallpaper design, you need to save it. Click on *Save As...* in Paintbrush's *File* menu. Give your wallpaper a filename with a .BMP extension. Put it in the directory on your hard disk called windows and save it. Close Paintbrush by double-clicking in its control-menu box.

Redecorating

To "paste" your wallpaper onto your desktop, open Control Panel and double-click on the Desktop icon. In the Wallpaper section, open the *File* list and select your newly named wallpaper file in the windows directory. When you click *OK*, your design will appear on screen.

Greetings and invitations

Use Paintbrush to create pictures you can mount on cardboard to make greetings cards and party invitations.

Getting started

Open Paintbrush and select *Image Attributes...* in the *Options* menu. Specify a canvas that is about 12cm wide and 17cm high. Click *OK* and your canvas will appear.

When you draw your picture, use the scroll bars (see page 16) to fill the whole of your canvas.

Some pictures drawn in Paintbrush

Outlined shapes

If you don't have a printer that prints in colour, create a design made up of outlined shapes that you can colour in after the picture is printed out. These are the icons for the tools which create outlined shapes.

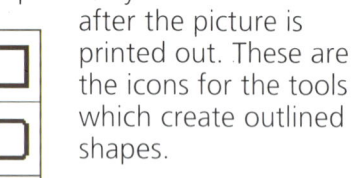

A section of Paintbrush's Toolbox

Give your shapes a clear outline by selecting a wide tool width in the Linesize box.

This picture uses many of the outline tools.

Lettering in Paintbrush

This is the icon for the Text tool. You can use it to add text to a picture. There is a selection of different fonts, text sizes and styles to choose from. (You can read more about fonts and styles on page 14.)

To add text to a picture, select the Text tool. Open the *Text* menu and you will see the options of *Bold*, *Italic* or *Underline*. If you select *Fonts...*, a dialog box will appear in which you can alter the font and size of your text. Click on your canvas and start typing.

You could make a card using different fonts and sizes.

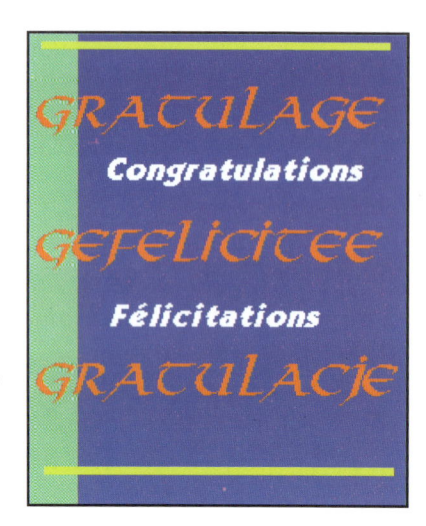

Mistakes

If you want to change some text in a Paintbrush picture, use the Eraser tool to rub it out and then start again.

If you make a mistake while you are typing, you can use the back-space key to erase the mistake, then retype your text correctly.

20

Zoom in

If you want to draw a picture carefully and precisely, try using a technique called "zooming in".

When you select *Zoom In* in the *View* menu, your pointer becomes a rectangle. Move this rectangle to the area of your picture you want a closer look at. Click, and the display will change to show that area in more detail.

When you are ready, select *Zoom Out* in the *View* menu to go back to the normal view of your canvas.

Making changes

This is the Brush tool's icon. When you have zoomed in on an area of a picture, you can use this tool to add detail to your picture, square by square. If you want to correct a mistake in a picture, add squares of the background colour by clicking in the squares with your right-hand mouse button.

Looking at a detail of a picture using Zoom In

This box shows you the area you are altering, at its normal size.

The magnified area of your canvas

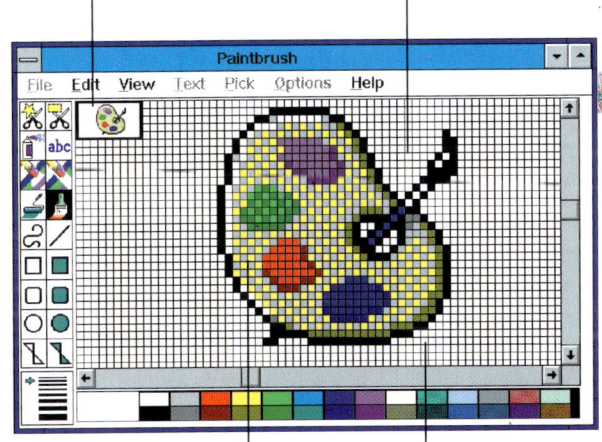

Click on each square or drag your pointer over them to add colour.

Add background colour if you want to delete mistakes.

Finishing touches

When the picture for your greetings card is finished, select *Save As...* in the *File* menu. Give your file a name (say, card.bmp), place it in the projects directory and save it.

Print out your picture onto a piece of paper. Mount it on a piece of cardboard that has been folded in half. Use paints, coloured pencils or felt tips to colour it in.

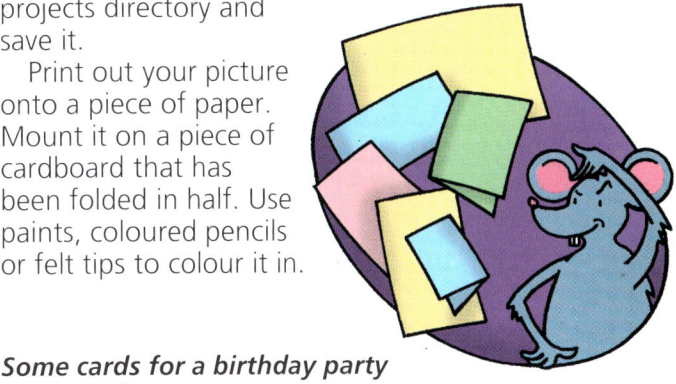

Some cards for a birthday party

The personal touch

Many companies have a symbol or picture, called a "logo", which helps people to identify them or their products. Using Paintbrush you can create your own distinctive logo.

Creating a logo

Open a copy of Paintbrush by double-clicking on its icon in Program Manager. Select *Image Attributes...* in the *Options* menu. Create a canvas about 4cm in width and 4cm in height, and then click *OK*. Now draw your logo, using any of the tools and paints.

Here is a selection of different logo ideas.

When you have created your logo, select *Save As...* in the *File* menu, give your file a name (say, logo.bmp), place it in the projects directory and save it.

Some logos on letterheads and personal cards

Using your logo

You could add your logo to the letterhead you created on page 13. Open the Paintbrush file containing your logo and select the Scissor tool.

This is the Scissor tool icon.

Use it to draw a dotted line around your logo, as shown below. Select *Copy* from the *Edit* menu. Close this copy of Paintbrush by double-clicking in its control-menu box.

Cutting out your logo

The cutting line created by the Scissor tool

This is the area that will be cut out.

Inserting a logo

Open your letterhead file and click your pointer at the top of the page. Select *Paste* from the *Edit* menu. When your logo appears, highlight it and use the commands in the *Paragraph* menu (see page 13) to position it in the middle of your page, or on the left- or right-hand side. In a Write document, text can't appear on the same line as a picture.

Personal Cards

A great way to give people your address and telephone number is on a personal card. To make one, open a copy of Paintbrush. Select *Image Attributes...* in the *Options* menu and specify a canvas that is about 9cm wide and 5.5cm high.

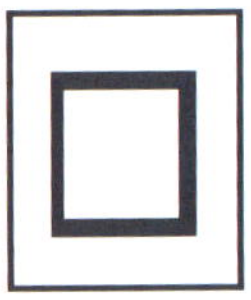

This is the icon for the Rectangle tool. Use it to draw a rectangle around the edge of your canvas to form an outline. Paste a copy of your logo onto the card using the technique described on page 22. Type in your address and phone number using the Text tool.

When you have finished, select *Save As...* in the *File* menu. Give your file a name, place it in the projects directory and save it.

Here is a sample card.

Cards galore

By copying your personal card a number of times, you can produce a printed sheet of cards that you can cut out and give to your friends. Open the file containing your card and use the Pick tool to cut around it. Select *Copy* in the *Edit* menu.

This is the Pick tool icon.

Next, you need to create a new canvas to paste your card onto. Select *Image Attributes...* in the *Options* menu and create a canvas about 20cm wide and 18cm high. When the canvas appears select *Zoom Out* in the *View* menu.

Your whole canvas will appear in the Paintbrush window. Select *Paste* in the *Edit* menu. A rectangle with crossed lines on it will appear. Click your pointer on the canvas outside this rectangle and a copy of your card will appear. If you select *Paste* again, a new rectangle will appear on top of your card. Click and drag this rectangle into position beside your first card.

Placing six cards onto a canvas

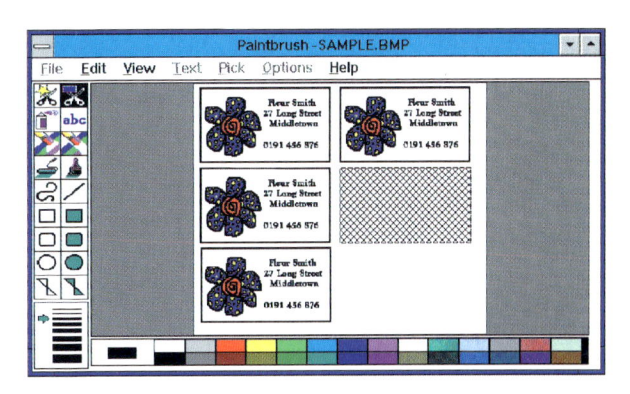

Repeat this process until you have six cards on your canvas. Now select *Zoom In* in the *View* menu. Select *Save As...* in the *File* menu. Give your file a new name (say, sixcard.bmp), place it in the projects directory and save it.

Printing out

Print out the file with your six cards onto a piece of paper. You can use colourful paper or use pens and paints to add colour to your cards.

Glue the paper to a sheet of thin cardboard. When it is dry, carefully cut out the cards.

Decorate your card with pens, pencils or paints.

Outlines and stencils

With Paintbrush's Text tool you can create outlined letters. Print them out and colour them in, or make them into stencils to decorate your possessions.

Outlined letters

To create outlined text, open a copy of Paintbrush and select the Text tool. In the *Text* menu, choose the font, size and style of the text you want to use. Also in the *Text* menu, select *Bold* and *Outline* so that tick marks appear beside them.

Paintbrush's Text menu

Text	
Regular	
√ Bold	Ctrl+B
Italic	Ctrl+I
Underline	Ctrl+U
√ Outline	
Shadow	
Fonts...	

Choose white as your foreground colour and black as your background colour. Type in some outlined letters using the keyboard. When you have finished, change your background colour to white and foreground colour to black.

A sample of outlined text

ABCDE

Thicker letters

To make the outlines of your letters thicker, drag a rectangle around your letters with the Pick tool. Select *Copy* in the *Edit* menu and then select *Paste*. A copy of your letters will appear in the top left-hand corner of your canvas.

A copy of your lettering

ABCDE
ABCDE

With your pointer, drag this copy almost exactly over the top of the other letters. You will see that when it is almost, but not quite, over the top, the letters look twice as thick. Release your mouse button to position the letters.

ABCDE

The copy is right beside the original.

If the letters of your text are too close together, use the Scissor tool to cut carefully around each one. Click on it, and drag it slightly away from its neighbour.

What is a stencil?

A stencil is a design that is cut into paper or plastic. You dab paint into the cutout shape to leave a pattern when the stencil is lifted off.

You can use outlined letters created in Paintbrush to make a stencil to decorate a folder, a pencil tin or a mug.

Some of the things you can decorate with stencils.

Making a stencil

First measure the size of the area you want to stencil. Open a copy of Paintbrush, and select *Image Attributes...* in the *Options* menu. Specify a canvas that is the same size as the area you want to stencil. Now, when you design your stencil, you will be able to see exactly how much of the object it will cover.

When you have finished your stencil design, select *Save As...* in the *File* menu. Give the file a filename (stencil.bmp for example), place it in your projects directory and save it.

Printing out

Print out your file onto the thickest paper you can use in your printer. Stencils get soggy when you use paint on them, so the thicker the paper, the longer they will last.

On this page, you can find out how to use a Paintbrush stencil to decorate the lid of a pencil tin.

Stencilling

To stencil the lid of a pencil tin, you will need the following things: a sponge or crumpled cloth, ceramic paints, a piece of clear book-covering film, masking tape, a pencil tin, a ruler and an old saucer.

This is what you do:

1. Measure the lid of your tin and specify a canvas in Paintbrush that is the same size as it. Type your name in outlined type.

This canvas is the same size as the tin's lid.

2. Print out your name onto a piece of paper. Cut a piece of book-covering film that is slightly smaller than the lid of the tin. Tape the film over the letters on your print-out.

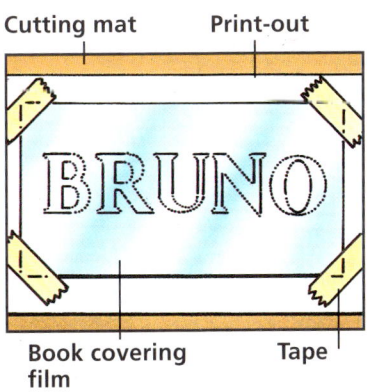

Cutting mat **Print-out**

Book covering film **Tape**

3. Using a craft knife, cut out all the letters. Make sure you cut through both the print-out paper and the book-covering film.

Smooth out edges as you cut.

4. Separate the print-out and the film and stick the film onto the tin. Add any middle parts of letters.

5. Put some paint onto the saucer. Dip the sponge into it, dab it on a paper towel, then over the letters.

6. Peel off the film carefully when the paint is dry.

25

All change

The Paintbrush application allows you to alter pictures by adding details to them and making them larger or smaller.

Dressing up

You can make different costumes for a figure drawn in Paintbrush. Open a copy of Paintbrush and draw a basic body shape. When you are ready, select *Save As...* in the *File* menu. Give your file a name (say, body.bmp), place it in your projects directory and save it.

A basic body shape in Paintbrush, ready to be altered

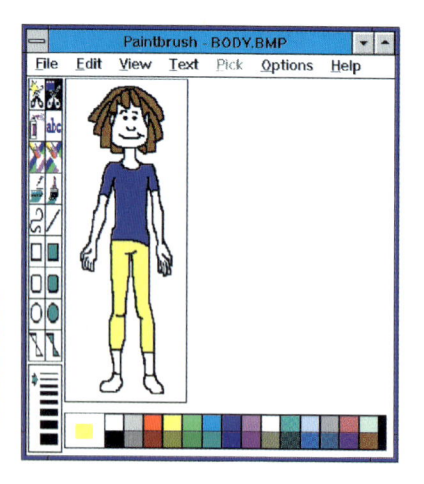

All change

Draw an outfit for your figure. Select *Save As...* in the *File* menu. Give your file a new name (such as clown.bmp) and place it in your projects directory. This ensures that your body.bmp file remains unaltered.

To design another outfit, select *Open...* in the *File* menu and highlight the body.bmp file in your projects directory. Click *OK* and your basic body will reappear.

Finishing touches

Print out your pictures onto paper. Glue thin pieces of cardboard to the back of the print-outs. When the glue is dry, use a sharp pair of scissors or a craft knife to cut around your figures. If you don't have a colour printer, use crayons or paints to colour in the clothes.

To make a figure stand up, glue a triangular piece of cardboard to the back of it.

A selection of figures you could make

Badges

You can use Paintbrush to design a selection of badges. Try making the logo you drew on page 22 into a badge. To find your logo, open Paintbrush and in the *File Name* list, highlight your logo.bmp file in the projects directory and click OK. The file will open.

Draw around your logo with the Pick tool and select *Copy* in the *Edit* menu. Now select *New* in the *File* menu. When a new canvas appears on your screen select *Image Attributes...* in the *Options* menu. Click on the *Default* button and then select OK. Finally select *Paste* in the *Edit* menu and a copy of your logo will appear on the canvas.

Some badge designs based on logos

Shrink and grow

In your new Paintbrush file you can change the size and shape of your logo. With the Pick tool draw a rectangle around it. Select *Shrink + Grow* in the *Pick* menu. Your pointer will change into a cross-shaped cursor. Move it to a clear area of your canvas. Click the cursor on the canvas and drag a rectangular shape. When you release your mouse button, a copy of your logo will appear.

Using Shrink + Grow

A picture

To make the picture bigger, drag a large rectangle.

To shrink it, draw a small rectangle.

These badges have been coloured in with felt-tip pens.

Undistorted

When you use *Shrink + Grow*, you can drag out a rectangle of any size and shape, and your logo will change to fill it. However, to make sure that your logo is not distorted (which means stretched too wide or too narrow), hold down the Shift key while you drag out the rectangle.

Making badges

When you are happy with the size and shape of the logo for your badge, select *Save As...* in the *File* menu. Give your file a name (say, badge.bmp) place it in the projects directory and save it.

Print out your badge file onto a piece of paper. Glue a piece of thin cardboard to the back of the paper. Cut out your badge and colour it, as in the previous project.

To make your badge more hard-wearing, you could cover it with some clear book-covering film.

Use sticky tape to attach a safety pin to the back of the badge.

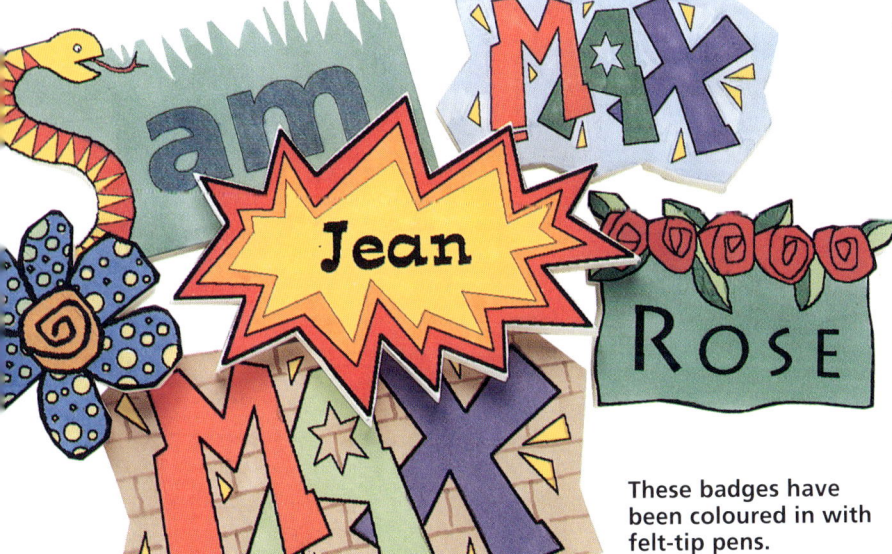

Mouse mats

When using a computer mouse, you need to have a clean, flat surface to work on. You can buy a special mouse mat, or make your own using the Paintbrush application.

Here are some ideas for mouse mats to make.

A graffiti mat

To create a mat with your name written on it like graffiti on a wall, open a copy of Paintbrush and maximize it to fill your screen. Select *Page Setup...* in the *File* menu. A dialog box appears. In the Margins section enter "0" for the *Top*, *Bottom*, *Left* and *Right* margins and click *OK*.

Select *Image Attributes...* in the *Options* menu and in the dialog box, specify a canvas 7cm wide and 10cm high. Then click *OK*.

Brick laying

Select the Rectangle tool and choose white as your foreground colour and black as your background colour. In the top left-hand corner of your canvas area draw a brick.

The Rectangle tool icon

Select the Roller tool and choose a pale colour as your foreground colour. Click the inside of your brick to fill it with paint.

The Roller tool icon

Creating a brick wall

To create a wall of bricks, use the Pick tool to cut around your brick. Select *Copy* in the *Edit* menu and then *Paste*. A new brick will appear on top left-hand corner of the canvas.

Drag the brick into position beside the first brick, with a small gap between them. Repeat this process until you have a full row of bricks.

Copying rows of bricks

When you select *Zoom Out* in the *View* menu, your whole canvas will appear in the Paintbrush window. Use the Pick tool to draw around the row of bricks. Select *Copy* in the *Edit* menu and then select *Paste*.

A block covered with crossed lines will appear. Drag this box underneath your first row of bricks. When it is in position, click your cursor on the canvas outside the block. A new row of bricks will appear.

Select *Paste* again for another row of bricks to position and gradually fill your canvas with rows of bricks.

Copying a row of bricks

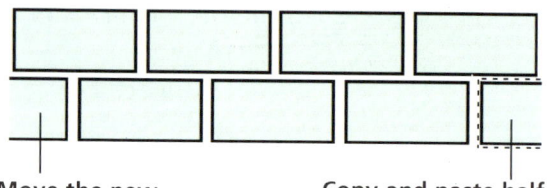

Move the new row of bricks across half a brick.

Copy and paste half a brick into the space at the end of each row.

Writing on the wall

Select a wide width in the Line Width box and, with the Eraser tool, write your name across the wall. Add any decoration you like. Select *Save As...* in the *File* menu. Give your file a name, place it in the projects directory and save it.

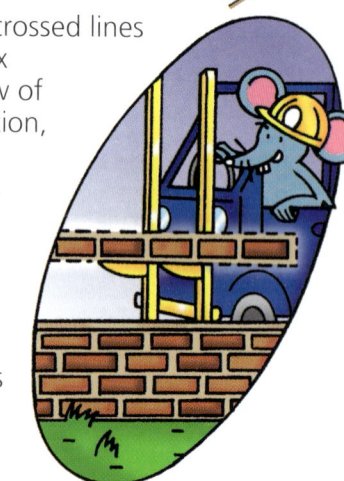

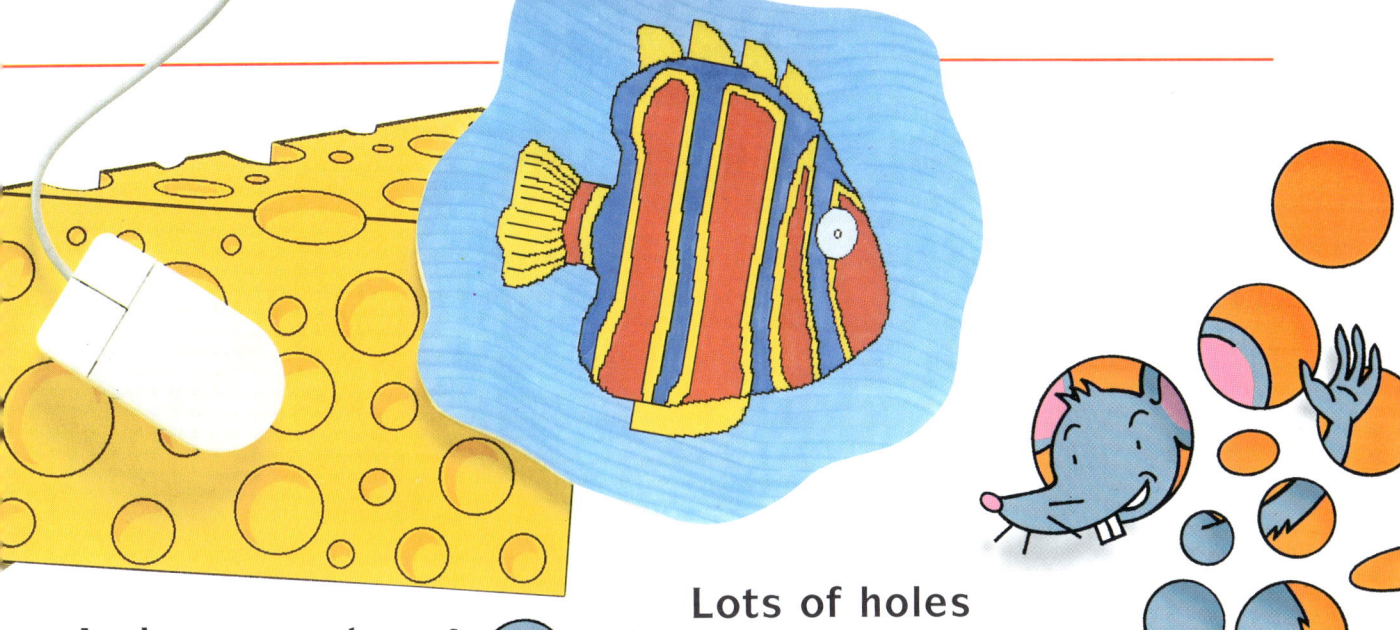

A cheese mat

To make a cheese mat, open a copy of Paintbrush. Specify a canvas in the same way as described for the graffiti mat.

Use the Rectangle tool to draw a rectangle like the one in the picture below.

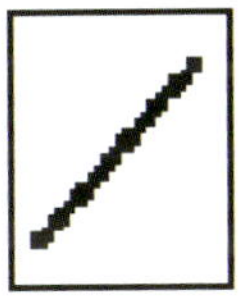

This is the icon for the Line tool. Use it to draw a line to form the top edge of the cheese.

Select the Curve Line tool icon and draw a line joining the top of the cheese to the rectangle. Use your cursor to curve the line. This is difficult. If you go wrong, select *Undo* in the *Edit* menu.

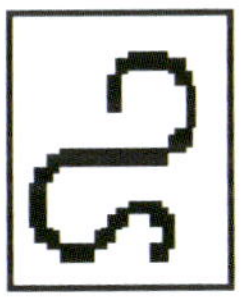

This is what the finished cheese will look like.

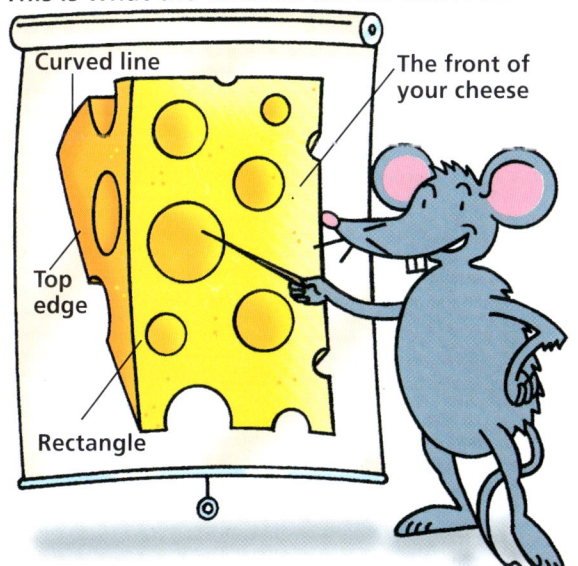

- Curved line
- The front of your cheese
- Top edge
- Rectangle

Lots of holes

Use the Circle tool to draw holes in your cheese. The holes on the front of the cheese should be perfect circles. If you hold down the Shift key while you drag, you will get a circle. The holes on the top of the cheese should be squashed circles, called ellipses. You can draw them by dragging wide circles with your cursor.

An ellipse
A circle

On the edge

Make sure that some of the circles you draw extend over the edge of the cheese. Where they fall outside the cheese, use the Eraser tool to rub out part of the circle and the edge.

Finishing touches

When your picture is ready, select *Print*... in the *File* menu. In the Print box specify 275% in the *Scaling* section. Print the file onto a piece of A4 paper (about 21cm wide and 30cm high). You could use a sheet of yellow paper for the cheese mat. Use paints or pens to add colour to the print-out.

Finally, glue the print-out onto a piece of cardboard and cover both cardboard and print-out in clear book-covering film.

29

Stickers and scenes

An aquarium filled with exotic fish, Photofit faces and fabulous fashion, are just some of the things you can create with a technique called clip-art. You will need to use the Paintbrush application.

What is clip-art

Clip-art is a method of transferring a set of pictures from one Paintbrush window to another. You can treat the pictures like reusable stickers, sticking them onto different scenes and using them in different combinations.

Two copies of Paintbrush

To tackle a clip-art project, you need two copies of Paintbrush open at once. First, open one copy of Paintbrush by double-clicking on its icon in Program Manager. Use your cursor to re-size (see page 5) this window until it covers the top half of your screen.

Go back to Program Manager and open another copy of Paintbrush by double-clicking on its icon again. Re-size this window to fill the bottom half of your screen.

Active window

When you have two copies of the Paintbrush window open, click on the window you want to work on and it will become active, which means it is ready to use. The other window, which is not being used, is called inactive.

Making stickers

Maximize one of the Paintbrush windows to fill your screen. Draw a selection of pictures, say a group of fish. This will be your stickers canvas.

A selection of stickers

Make sure the stickers are small, so that they can fit into a scene.

When you have finished, select *Save As...* in the *File* menu, give this Paintbrush file a name, place it in the projects directory and save it. Click the Restore button of this Paintbrush window.

Setting a scene

Now create a scene for your stickers to appear in. Maximize your second Paintbrush window. Make sure that the background colour you select for this canvas is the same as that chosen for your stickers canvas. Design a scene.

This is your scenery canvas. Select *Save As...* in the *File* menu, give the file a name, place it in the projects directory and save it. Click the Restore button of this Paintbrush window.

An aquarium scene

Copying and pasting

This is the icon for the Scissor tool. Use it to draw around one of the pictures on your stickers canvas. Select *Copy* in the *Edit* menu. In your scenery canvas, click the Maximize button and select *Paste* in the *Edit* menu. The sticker will appear on your canvas.

Click on the sticker and drag it into the position you want it. Then release the mouse button. Once you click anywhere outside the dotted line around your sticker, you won't be able to move it again.

Move your stickers into position in your scene.

All change

You can vary the size of your stickers, as in the picture above, by using the "Shrink and Grow" technique described on page 27.

To make a sticker point in another direction, draw around it with the Pick tool and select *Flip Horizontal* or *Flip Vertical* in the *Pick* menu.

This fish has been flipped vertically.

This one has been flipped horizontally.

When your clip-art picture is finished, select *Save As...* in the *File* menu, give the file a name, place it in the projects directory and save it.

More clip-art ideas

You can use clip-art in many different ways. Try producing disguises by adding a selection of hair, glasses and beard stickers to a basic face. Create your own alphabet or design a variety of outfits and accessories to mix and match on a model.

You can create a rogues gallery of criminals.

Design your own alphabet.

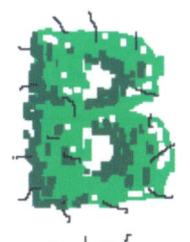

Design outfits with clip-art.

31

A picture address book

Using an application called Cardfile, you can create an address book to store on your computer. Add cheeky cartoon portraits of your friends to the cards, so that you laugh every time you look at them.

What is Cardfile?

Cardfile works like a pile of index cards that always remain stacked in alphabetical order. Open Cardfile by double-clicking on its icon in Program Manager.

This is the Cardfile icon.

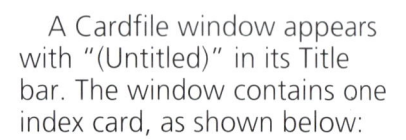

A Cardfile window appears with "(Untitled)" in its Title bar. The window contains one index card, as shown below:

This is a Cardfile window.

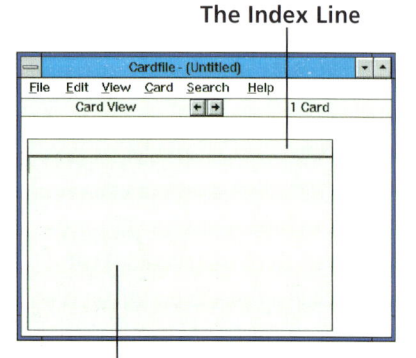

The Index Line

The main area of the card

It's a good idea to give your new cardfile a name straight-away. Select *Save As...* in the *File* menu. Give your file a filename with a .CRD extension. Place it in your projects directory and save it.

Filling the cards

To use the first card that appears when Cardfile opens, double-click in the Index Line area. An Index dialog box opens.

An Index dialog box

Type the name of one of your friends in the *Index Line* box. Put their surname first, because address books are usually arranged in alphabetical order according to surname. Then click *OK*.

To add an address and a telephone number, click in the main area of the card. A flashing cursor will appear and you can start typing.

Adding cards

To add a new card for each of your friends, press the F7 key. In the Index dialog box, type in another friend's name and click *OK*. A new card will appear at the top of your pile.

Face facts

Pictures added to the index cards will make your address book more colourful. Alternatively, you could add a map showing you how to find a friend's house.

You can draw pictures using Paintbrush and then paste them onto your address cards using the technique below.

Sizing

To prepare a canvas that is the correct size for your picture, minimize the Cardfile window. Open a copy of Paintbrush by double-clicking on its icon. In the *Options* menu select *Image Attributes...*

In the dialog box that appears, make sure that you are working in centimetres by selecting cm in the *Units* section. Enter a size of about 6cm in the width box and 6cm in the height box. Then click *OK* and close that copy of Paintbrush by double-clicking in its control-menu box.

Creating a picture

Return to your Cardfile window by double-clicking on its icon at the foot of your screen. Choose the card of one of your friends. Bring it to the front of the pile by clicking on its Index Line. You can also use the arrows below the Cardfile Menu bar to flick through your cards. This is what the arrows look like.

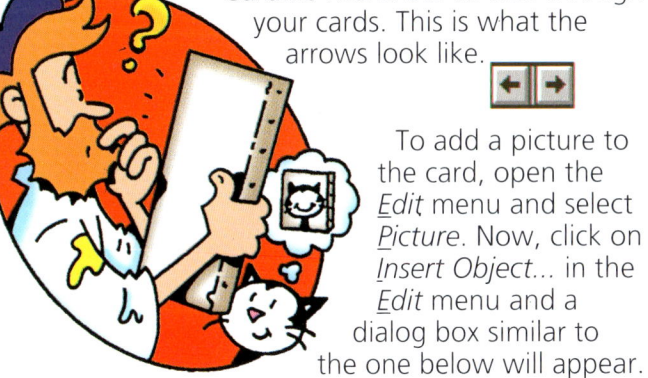

To add a picture to the card, open the *Edit* menu and select *Picture*. Now, click on *Insert Object...* in the *Edit* menu and a dialog box similar to the one below will appear.

An Insert New Object dialog box

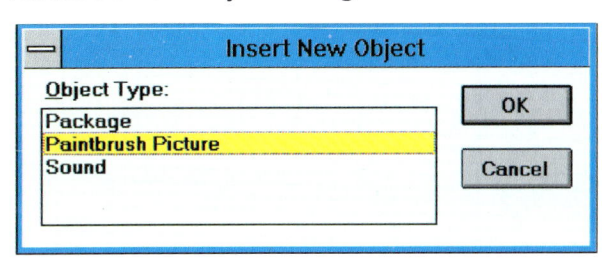

Select *Paintbrush Picture* in the *Object Type* list. When you click *OK*, a Paintbrush window will open containing a correctly sized canvas. Now you are ready to draw a picture.

A cartoon picture on a canvas in Paintbrush

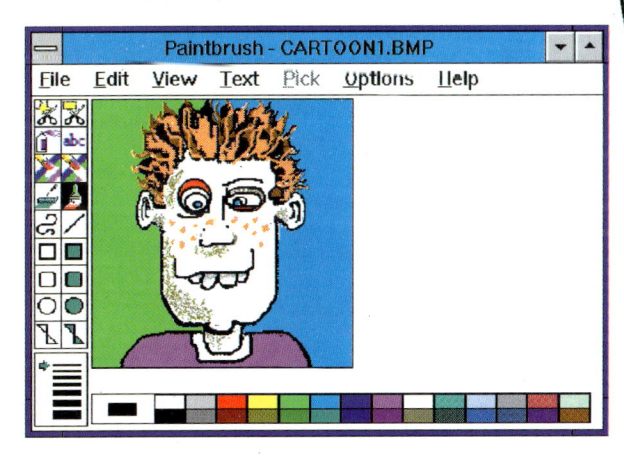

Inserting a picture

When you have completed your picture, select *Update* in Paintbrush's *File* menu. Click on *Exit & Return to...* in the *File* menu. The picture will appear on your index card. Drag it into position.

Each card can have an address and a picture.

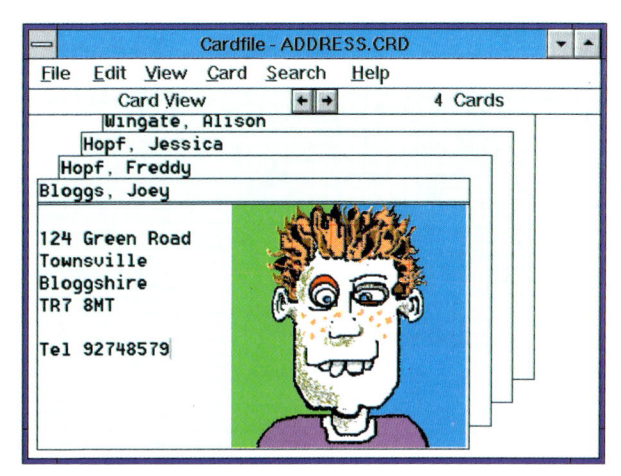

All change

It's easy to alter an index card if one of your friends moves home or even grows a beard. To change text, select *Text* in Cardfile's *Edit* menu. Alter the name at the top of a card by double-clicking in the Index Line area. A dialog box appears. Make your changes and click *OK*. To alter an address, click in the main area of the card and type in your changes.

To change a picture, select *Picture* in the *Edit* menu. Double-click on the picture you want to alter and a copy of Paintbrush will open. When you have made your alterations, click on *Update* in the *File* menu. Finally, Click on *Exit and Return to...* in the *File* menu.

Whenever you add a new card to your cardfile or change an existing card, save the cardfile before closing it. To do this, select *Save* in the *File* menu.

33

Character maps and codes

You can use your computer to send baffling, coded messages. People won't be able to understand these messages until you explain how to decode them using a Windows application called Character Map.

What is a character?

Any letter, number or symbol that your computer can produce is called a character. Each font (see page 14) has up to 256 different characters. This book is printed in a font called Frutiger 45. So, 3, m, @ and # are all characters in that particular font.

Character Maps

This is the icon for the Character Map application. When you open it, by double-clicking on the icon in Program Manager, a window like the one below appears. It contains a map of all the characters available in one of the fonts stored on your computer.

There are different maps for each of the fonts. To look at the different maps, open the *Font* list and highlight the name of another font. The character map will change to show all the characters available in that particular font.

This is the Character Map window showing the map of a font called Times.

This is the name of the font to which all the characters in this map belong.

In this window appears a list of any characters you select.

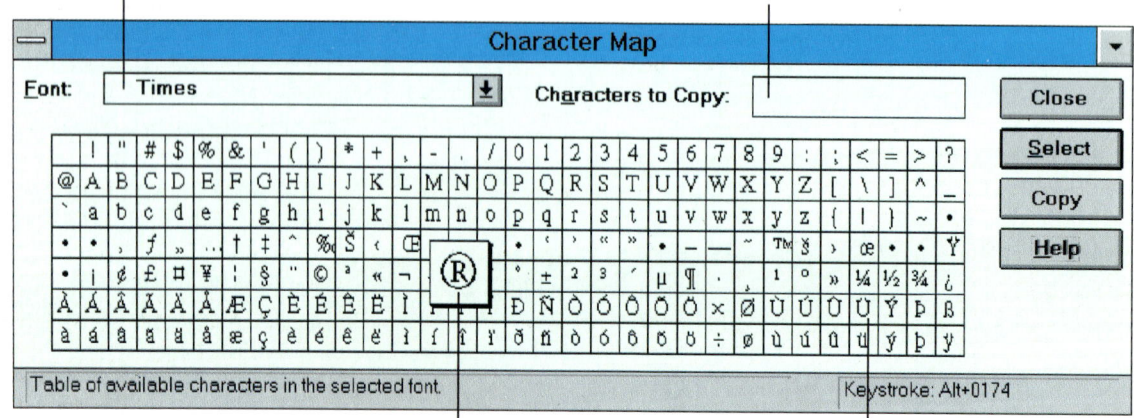

This character has been magnified using the pointer.

Each square contains a different character.

A closer look

The character map squares are very small and it can be difficult to see the exact shape of some of the characters. To take a closer look at any character in the map, click on its square and hold down your mouse button. As you click, the square will appear magnified.

34

Coded messages

To write a coded message, open a copy of Write by double-clicking on its icon in Program Manager. In the *Character* menu select *Fonts...* Select the font called Arial and click *OK*.

Now type into your Write document the secret message you want to send.

Use the cursor to highlight your message. Select *Fonts...* in the *Character* menu again and choose the font called Symbol. Symbol has lots of strange characters.

This is a coded message in Symbol. Find out how to decode it below.

Αγεντ Τινκερβελλ
Χομε ανδ φινδ με
ουτσιδε Πηαραοη
Τυτ σ πψραμιδ ατ
μιδνιγητ τονιγητ.
Ι ωιλλ βε δισγυισεδ
ασ α χαμελ οωνερ.
Τηε πασσωορδ ισ
Οκλαηομα.
Σιγνεδ

Αγεντ Οβϖιουσ

To make sure that your message is large enough to read easily when it is printed out, select 14 in the *Size* list in the Fonts dialog box.

Now choose *OK* and your message will be instantly transformed into a mysterious collection of symbols.

Sending your message

To save your message, select *Save As...* in the *File* menu. Give your file a name, place it in the projects directory and save it. Print out this file onto a piece of paper and send it to a friend. Close the Write window by double-clicking in its control menu box.

Remember, your friend must have a computer that has Windows software installed, in order to translate your message.

Tell your friend

Let your friend try and puzzle out the code for a while, but then reveal some clues about how to decode it.

Say that your message is written in Symbol and that using the Character Map application is the only way to decipher it.

Time to decode

This is what your friend needs to do to decode the message. Open Character Map and select Symbol in the *Font* list. Starting with the first character in your message, use the pointer to move around the map, looking for a character that exactly matches the one in your message.

When your friend finds the right character, he or she should double-click on the square in which the character appears. The symbol will appear in the *Character to Copy* box, like the one below.

Ch**a**racters to Copy: Αγεντ Οβϖιουσ

Your friend should work through in this way, not forgetting to put in spaces where they appear in your message.

All is revealed

At the end of the message, your friend should click the *Copy* button. Close Character Map by double-clicking in its control menu box and open a copy of Write. Select *Fonts...* in the *Character* menu. In the *Font* list select the font called Arial and click *OK*. Finally, open Write's *Edit* menu and select *Paste*.

Your message will appear in the Write document decoded and ready to read.

Invent your own quiz game

You can create a Cardfile with quiz questions on each index card. Using an application called Object Packager, you can hide the answers on the cards. When you want to reveal an answer, all you have to do is double-click.

A quiz question on an index card

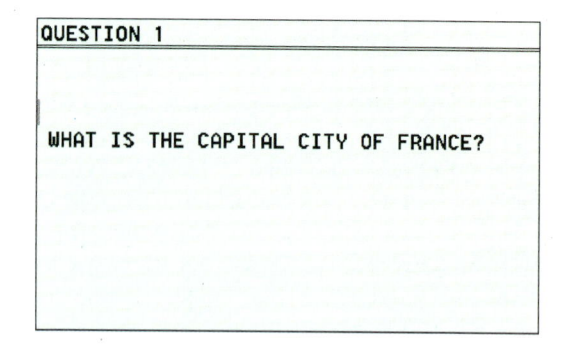

QUESTION 1

WHAT IS THE CAPITAL CITY OF FRANCE?

What is Object Packager?

This is the icon for Object Packager. This application "packages" up one file and inserts it into another. The file that is packaged up is called the object. It can be any kind of file, like a Paintbrush picture or a Write document. The file into which the object is inserted is called the destination file.

The object file appears in the destination file as an icon. When you double-click on this icon the object file automatically opens.

Questions and answers

To produce a quiz game, start by thinking up a selection of questions and answers. Following the instructions on page 32, create a Cardfile, give it a filename, place it in your projects directory and save it.

Open Cardfile's *Edit* menu and click on *Text*. On your first index card, type a number on the Index Line and a question on the main area of the card. Then minimize Cardfile.

Open a copy of Write and type in the answer to your question. Select *Save As...* in the *File* menu. Give your file a filename (answer1.wri for example), place it in your projects directory and save it.

Packaging an object

Now you need to package up the answer document and insert it into your index card. Open Object Packager by double-clicking on its icon in Program Manager. In the window, click on the word Content. Select *Import...* in the *File* menu. In the dialog box that opens, highlight answer1.wri in your projects directory and click *OK*.

The filename appears in the Content section of Object Packager's window and a Write icon appears in the Appearance section. Select *Copy Package* in the *Edit* menu and then close Object Packager by double-clicking in its control-menu box.

This is Object Packager's window containing a packaged Write file.

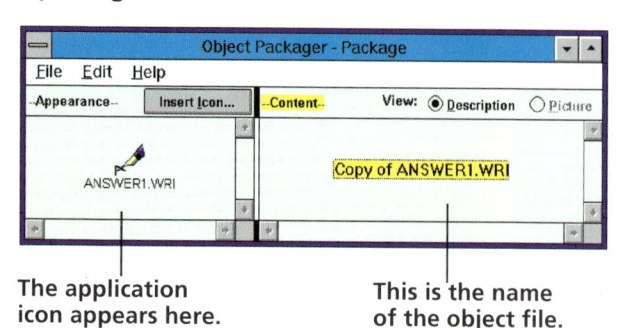

Object Packager - Package
File Edit Help
Appearance Insert Icon... Content View: ● Description ○ Picture
ANSWER1.WRI   Copy of ANSWER1.WRI

The application icon appears here.

This is the name of the object file.

Inserting an object

To insert an answer document into an index card, first maximize the Cardfile window. Open the *Edit* menu, select *Picture* so that a tick mark appears beside it. Select *Paste* in the *Edit* menu. A Write icon appears. Drag it into position.

To find out the answer to the question on the card, double-click on this icon. The Write document containing the answer opens. Close it when you have finished by double-clicking in its control-menu box. Repeat this process to add more question cards and answers to your cardfile.

An index card with a Write file packaged in it

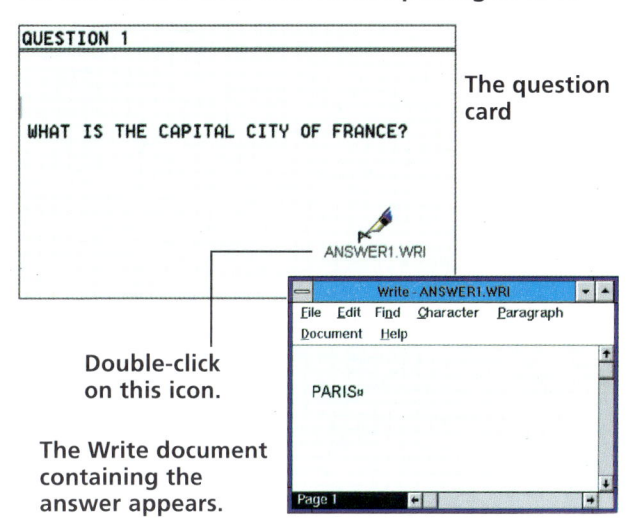

The question card

Double-click on this icon.

The Write document containing the answer appears.

Computer sound

Many computers can make sounds. Find out if your computer can by opening Control Panel. Double-click on the Sound icon.

This is the Sound icon.

In the dialog box that opens, there is a list of sound files. They have the filename extension .WAV.

If the files listed in the *Files* section appear dimmed (pale grey), it means that your computer can't make sounds. If they aren't dimmed, highlight one of them and click the *Test* button. You should hear a sound. If you do, you can use some of these sound files in your quiz game.

The Sound window with a list of .WAV files

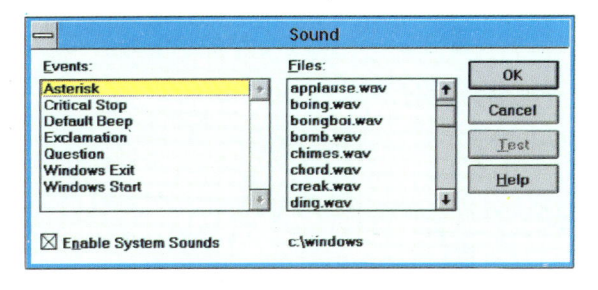

Adding sounds

Open Object Packager and select *Import...* in the *File* menu. In the dialog box that appears, select the directory called windows. In the *File Name* box, type *.WAV and press the Return key. A list of the .WAV files on your computer appears. You may have one called applause.wav. Highlight it in the *File Name* list, then click *OK*. If you don't have this file, choose another one. Finally, select *Copy Package* in the *Edit* menu.

Close Object Packager and open your cardfile. Double-click on the Write icon on one of your cards to open an answer file. When it appears, position your cursor at the end of the text and select *Paste* in the *Edit* menu. A Sound icon will appear. Select *Save* in the *File* menu to ensure that the Sound file is saved in your Write file.

Now, if you get the answer right, double-click on this Sound icon and you will hear a round of applause.

Finding a hidden message

Using Object Packager, you can hide a secret file in an innocent-looking letter. Only your friends will know how to reveal the hidden information.

The picture at the bottom of the letter below looks pretty innocent. But when you double-click on it, a Paintbrush file opens revealing a less flattering portrait.

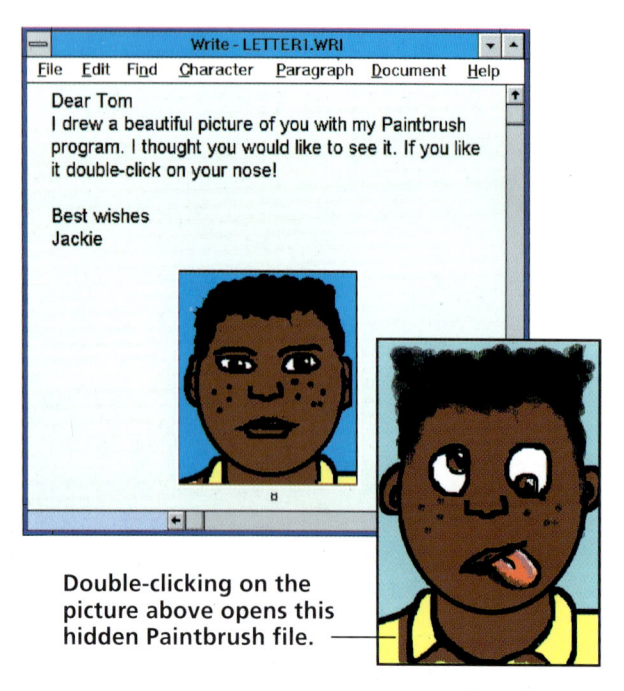

Double-clicking on the picture above opens this hidden Paintbrush file.

An innocent letter

First, you need to create a letter in which to hide a secret file. Open Write by double-clicking on its icon in Program Manager. In the Write window, type a letter. When you have finished, minimize the Write window so that it appears as an icon at the bottom of your screen.

Compiling a secret file

Next, open Paintbrush and draw a secret picture. When you have finished, select *Save As...* in the *File* menu. Give your file a name (say, secret.bmp), place it in your projects directory and save it. Close Paintbrush by double-clicking in its control menu box.

Packaging secrets

Open Object Packager and click on the Content section. Select *Import...* in the *File* menu. In the dialog box that appears, highlight the secret information file (secret.bmp) in your projects directory. When you click *OK*, the filename will appear in the Content section and a Paintbrush icon in the Appearance section.

Creating a disguise

Next, you need to disguise the icon in which your secret document is packaged. Click on the Object Packager's Appearance section and select *Cut* in the *Edit* menu. Minimize Object Packager and open a new copy of Paintbrush. Select *Paste* in the *Edit* menu. The icon from the Appearance section will appear on your canvas. Use the Eraser tool to rub it out.

In its place, draw an innocent-looking picture that will fit on your letter. Then, using the Scissor tool, cut around it. Select *Copy* in the *Edit* menu.

Close Paintbrush by double-clicking in its control-menu box. You don't need to save this file.

Hiding the evidence

Maximize Object Packager, and select *Paste* in the *Edit* menu. Your secret picture will appear in the Appearance section. Select *Copy Package* in the *Edit* menu and close Object Packager by double-clicking in its control-menu box.

The Paintbrush icon is replaced by your picture in Object Packager.

Maximize the Write file containing your letter. Place your cursor at the bottom of the text. Then select *Paste* in the *Edit* menu and the picture will appear.

To save the letter and the hidden file, select *Save As...* in Write's *File* menu. Give your file a name (say letter1.wri), place it in your projects directory and save it.

All is revealed

To reveal the hidden file, all you need to do is double-click on the picture at the bottom of your letter. The Paintbrush file containing your secret picture will open automatically. To close it, double-click in its control-menu box.

Sending your letter

To send this letter to a friend, copy the letter1.wri file onto a floppy disk. To do this, put a floppy disk in your computer's floppy disk drive. Open File Manager, which has an icon like this. Close all but one of the windows inside the File Manager window. Select *Select Drive...* in the *Disk* menu and in the dialog box that appears select the hard disk drive (usually labelled as the C drive).

A list of the directories on your hard disk will appear in the left-hand side of the window. Find your projects directory and double-click on it.

A list will appear in the right-hand side of the window. Click on your letter1.wri and drag it over to the symbol in the top left-hand corner of the window that looks like this.

This is your floppy disk drive. Release the mouse button. To check that your file has been copied onto the floppy disk, click your pointer on this symbol once. The name of your file will appear in the right-hand side of the window.

Who does this belong to?

You could set up a picture like the one below. Each character has a picture hidden in it. When you double-click on each character, you can find out who the tutu belongs to.

Double click here   **Double-click here**

Unlikely!   **That's more like it.**

39

Interactive storytime

Most stories have a beginning, a middle, and an end. Their plots never change. But with an "interactive" story, you can decide what happens next by making a series of choices. An interactive story has several possible plots and endings. Using Cardfile, you can write a story that will be different every time you read it.

Make sure that *Picture* is selected in the *Edit* menu and then select *Paste* in the *Edit* menu. When your picture appears, drag it to position.

Planning your story

To get an idea of how an interactive story works, look at the example on page 41. You need to create a series of index cards, each containing an event and two possible courses of action. Depending on which course you choose, you are directed to another numbered card, where the story continues. By making choices in this way, the plot develops.

Interactive stories are quite difficult to write, so plan your story first. You can make it as complex as you like, with as many cards and choices as you like. Make sure, however, that you include a selection of cards with different endings to your story.

Adding sounds

If your computer can make sounds (see page 37), you can use Object Packager to add sound files to your index cards. Follow the technique described on page 37.

To increase the number of sound files you have to choose from, you can use a piece of software called the Microsoft® Sound Driver. It is a floppy disk that holds a selection of sound files which you can copy onto your computer.

Jumping between cards

To move from one card to another, click on the Index Line of the card you want. Alternatively, press the F4 key on the top row of your keyboard. A dialog box appears. Type in the number of the card you require and click OK. That card will jump to the top of your pile.

This is the Go To dialog box.

Type the card number here.

Creating a story cardfile

To find out how to create a cardfile, look at page 32. Give each index card a number on its Index Line and add the events and choices in your story to the main area of the card.

You can add pictures to some of your cards if you like. To do this, open a copy of Paintbrush. Draw a picture and select the Pick tool to cut it out.

Select *Cut* in the *Edit* menu, and then close Paintbrush without saving the file. Open your Cardfile and click on the card that you want to paste your picture onto.

40

Playing the game

When you are ready to read your story, make sure *Picture* has a tick beside it in Cardfile's *Edit* menu. This will ensure that when you double-click on a Sound icon on a card you will be able to hear the sound file play.

The story below is short and simple. You could set up an identical cardfile to give yourself an idea of how an interactive story works.

When you have written your own interactive story get people to read it. Watch them make choices. Were they the same as yours? They could even write some new index cards themselves to add a whole set of new adventures to the story.

These are some index cards that make up an interactive story.

1

A huge shark has torn a hole in the bottom of your boat. It is sinking fast and you are trapped in a cabin below the deck. [REDALERT.WAV]

What do you want to do now?
Go to card 2 to try and force open the jammed cabin door.
Go to card 3 to swim out of the hole made by the shark.

2

When you eventually manage to open the cabin door, a rush of sea water pours in, sweeping you back into the cabin. [CREAK.WAV]

What do you want to do now?
Go to card 3 to swim out through the hole made by the shark.
Go to card 4 to cling onto a table in the cabin.

3

As you swim out of the hole, the shark is waiting to attack you. It swims towards you menacingly.

What do you want to do now?
Go to card 5 to try and reach the lifeboat before the shark bites you.
Go to card 6 to stay and fight off the shark.

4

The engine room fills with water and the engine explodes. The blast throws you far away from the boat, but near to the shark. [BOMB.WAV]

What do you want to do now?
Go to card 5 to swim back toward the lifeboat.
Go to card 6 to swim toward land

5

You manage to reach the lifeboat before the shark attacks. With difficulty, you haul yourself safely on board. Only a couple of hours later, a rescue helicopter comes searching for you. You are winched aboard and flown home. When the newspapers hear your story, they buy it for £1000.

6

The shark swims away and you are able to swim to an island safely. You camp on a beach, waiting to be rescued; but it is six months before anyone finds you. When you finally get home, the newspapers hear of your adventure and pay you £100,000 for the story.

Macro magic

You can use an application called Recorder to record yourself drawing a picture in Paintbrush. Then watch as the picture magically redraws itself when you play back the recording. Recorder is a difficult application to use, so follow the instructions for this project carefully.

What is Recorder?

Recorder records the movements of your mouse and any keys that you press. It then plays back these actions. A recorded set of mouse movements and keystrokes is called a macro.

This is the icon for Recorder.

You can use Recorder like a video recorder. By recording the way in which a picture is drawn, Recorder can redraw the picture by playing back the recorded actions.

Preparations

To record yourself drawing a picture, open Paintbrush by double-clicking on its icon in Program Manager. Size the Paintbrush window to fill the top three-quarters of your screen. Select the Brush tool in the Toolbox. Make sure that the background colour selected is white and the foreground colour is black. Finally, minimize Paintbrush.

Using Recorder

In Program Manager, find the Recorder icon and double-click on it. When the Recorder window opens, select *Record...* in the *Macro* menu. In the dialog box that appears, make the same selections as shown in the following sample Record Macro dialog box.

A Record Macro dialog box

Give your macro a name here.

No cross in the *Continuous Loop* check box.

In the *Playback* section select *Fast*.

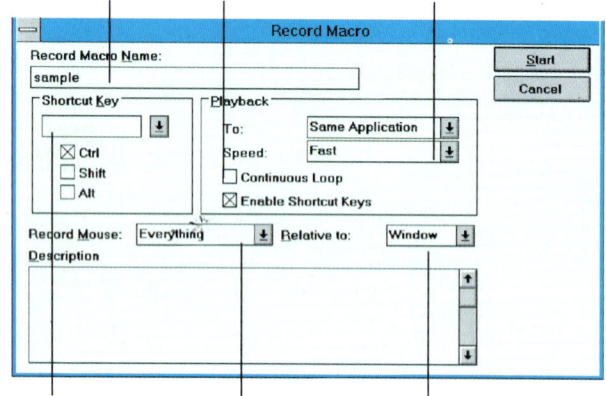

Leave this section blank.

In the *Record Mouse* section select *Everything*.

In the *Relative to* menu select *Window*.

Recording a macro

When you have entered these preferences, click the *Start* button. A flashing Recorder icon will appear at the bottom of your screen. This tells you that Recorder is recording. Double-click on the Paintbrush icon at the bottom of your screen and start to draw your picture.

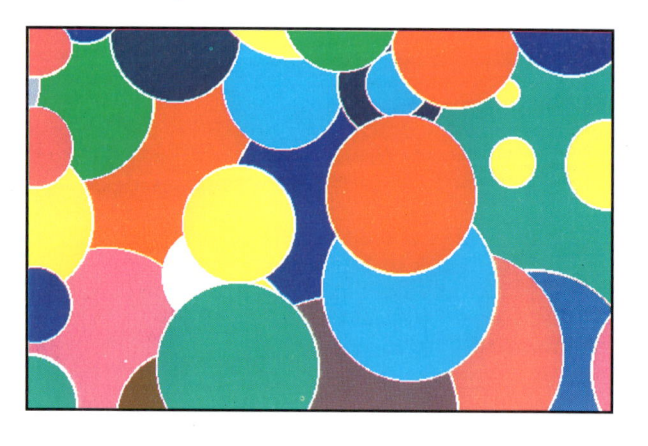

Simple patterns can look very effective.

42

Stop recording

To stop your recording when you have finished your picture, click once on the Recorder icon at the foot of your screen.

A Recorder dialog box will appear like the one below. Select *Save Macro* and then click *OK*.

This is the Recorder dialog box.

Preparing for playback

Recorder records the exact position of your pointer on screen. So before you play back a macro, make sure that all the objects on your screen are in the same position as they were before the macro was recorded. If you record a macro and then move, re-size or close windows, it won't play back.

In Paintbrush, make sure that the Brush tool is highlighted and that the background selected colour is white and the foreground colour is black.

Select *New...* in Paintbrush's *File* menu. A dialog box will appear asking "Do you want to save current changes?". Choose *No*. When a new canvas appears, minimize the Paintbrush window.

Playing a macro

To play back your macro, double-click on the Recorder icon. In the Recorder box, highlight the name of your macro and select *Run* in the *Macro* menu. Watch while your picture redraws itself.

Speed

You can play back a macro at two different speeds: fast or at the speed at which you recorded it.

To alter the speed, you have to change the selection in the *Playback* section of the Record Marco box before you record a new macro.

Saving macros

When you have recorded some macros, you can save them all in one file. Select *Save As...* in Recorder's *File* menu. Give your file a filename and a .REC extension. Finally, place it in the projects directory and save it.

Guessing games

There are lots of ways to use Recorder. Try playing the game below. In Recorder, select *Record...* in the *Macro* menu. In the dialog box, choose *Recorded Speed* in the *Playback* section.

Record a macro of drawing a picture. When you play it back, get your friends to try to guess what the picture is before it is complete.

A picture is revealed.

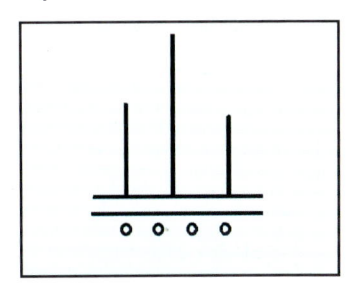

Can you guess what it is?

Now can you guess?

So that's what it is!

43

Cartoon fun

Using the Recorder application and a technique called clip-art, you can produce a simple but effective cartoon. This is a difficult project, so don't worry if you take some time to get it right. Follow the stages described below very carefully.

Scenes and characters

To prepare your cartoon, you need to draw a scene for the action to take place in, and a "character" to move around the scene.

Following the clip-art technique described on pages 30 and 31, open two copies of Paintbrush. Draw a scene on one canvas and a character on the other. Give each picture a different filename (say, scene.bmp and charcter.bmp). Place them both in your projects directory and save them.

This scenery canvas has an outer space setting with stars and planets.

This rocket is the character that will travel through the space scene.

Maximize the Paintbrush window containing your character. Use the Scissor tool to cut around it. Select *Copy* in the *Edit* menu. Now double-click in the control menu box to close this window.

Making preparations

Re-size you scenery canvas to fill the top three-quarters of your screen. Click on its Minimize button, so that it appears as an icon at the foot of your screen. This will ensure that when you restore this Paintbrush window, when you are recording your macro (see page 42), you have plenty of space to work in.

Setting up your recording

Open Recorder by double-clicking on its icon in Program Manager. Select *Record...* in the *Macro* menu. In the dialog box that appears, make the same selections as in the box shown on page 42. You could, however, select *Recorded Speed* in the *Playback* section, which is a better speed for playing back cartoons.

Shortcut keys

In the Record Macro dialog box there is a section called *Shortcut Key*. You can choose a code of two keys that, when pressed together, will automatically play back your macro.

If you want to use a shortcut key code, click in the box beside *Enable Shortcut Keys* until a cross appears. In the *Shortcut Key* box select a key from the drop-down list (say, F4). Next, place a cross in one of the boxes beside Ctrl, Shift or Alt (Ctrl, for example). This is your code.

The Shortcut Key and the Playback sections in the Record Macro dialog box

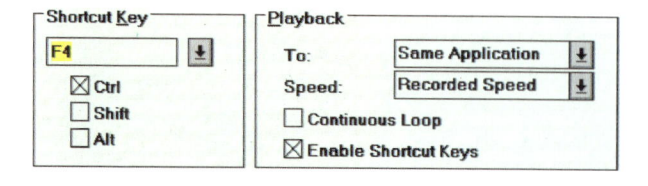

Recording your cartoon

To start recording your cartoon, click on *Start* in the Record Macro box. Double-click on the Paintbrush logo at the bottom of your screen and your scenery canvas will open.

Select *Paste* in the *File* menu and a copy of your character will appear in your scene. Drag it around your scene, to give the impression of the character moving.

You can move other characters in your scene. Cut them out and drag them. Be careful that you don't cut out part of the background too, or this will move around with your character.

Click on the Recorder icon at the bottom of your screen. The Recorder dialog box will appear. If you want to stop your recording completely, select *Save Macro* and click *OK*.

Resuming your recording

If you don't want to stop recording, but you want to have time to think about where to move a character next, you can just pause your recording. To do this, click on the Recorder icon.

When you are ready to continue recording, select *Resume Recording* in the Recorder dialog box and then click *OK*.

The Recorder dialog box

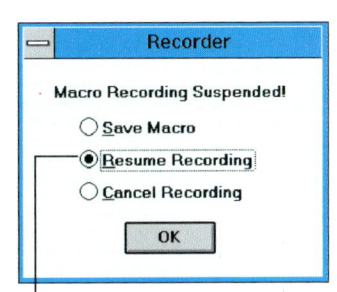

Resume Recording is selected.

Preparing for playback

Remember, before you play back your macro you must put everything back into the position it was in when you started recording.

Select *Open...* in the *File* menu of your scenery Paintbrush window. A box will appear asking you "Do you want to save current changes?". Select *No*. An Open dialog box appears. Highlight the name of your scenery file (scene.bmp) in the File *Name* menu and then click *OK*. Your scenery canvas will re-open, looking as it did before you started recording.

Make sure that the Brush tool is selected and that the foreground colour is black and the background colour is white. Finally, minimize your Paintbrush window.

A cartoon masterpiece

To play back your cartoon, hold down your two shortcut keys.

The following screens show another idea for a cartoon sequence:

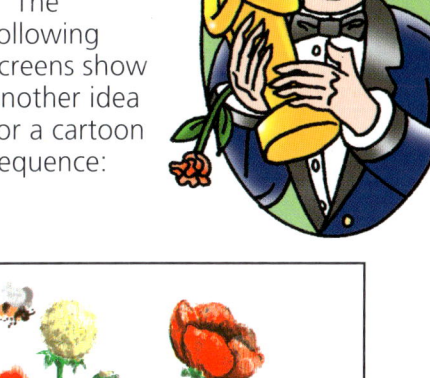

Cut around the bee with the Scissor tool and drag it around.

Make the bee bob from flower to flower.

Leave the bee, paste in a butterfly and float it around the flowers.

45

Windows® 95

Microsoft has developed a version of Windows called Windows 95. If you have this software installed on your computer, you can still complete many of the projects in this book.

These pages will tell you about some of the differences between Windows 95 and Windows 3.1, the version used in this book.

Starting Windows 95

When you switch on your computer and run the Windows 95 software, Program Manager doesn't appear on your screen. Instead a screen appears which includes a bar called a Taskbar. It contains a *Start* button like the one below.

Finding a program

To find a program stored on your computer, click the *Start* button. In the menu that appears, select *Programs*. Another menu will appear listing the program groups.

As you pass your pointer over the names of the program groups, further menus will open up, showing a list of the programs they contain.

Look through each group until you find the program you require.

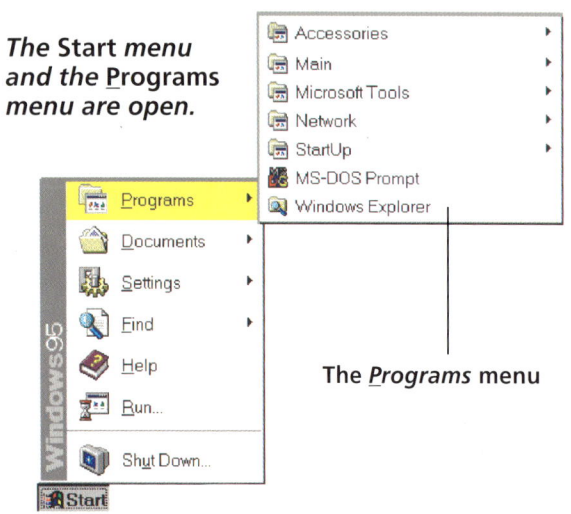

*The **Start** menu and the **Programs** menu are open.*

*The **Programs** menu*

Opening and closing programs

To open a program, double-click on its name in the menu. It will open in a window on your desktop. To close a program, select *Exit* in its *File* menu, or click once on the Close button in the top right-hand corner of the window.

A Windows 95 window

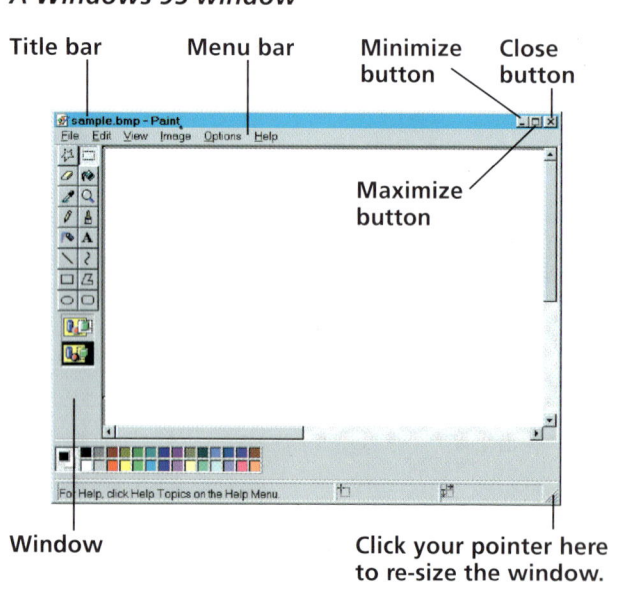

Title bar — Menu bar — Minimize button — Close button

Maximize button

Window — Click your pointer here to re-size the window.

Switching between programs

Whenever you open a program in Windows 95, a new button representing that program appears on the Taskbar.

To switch from one open program to another, simply click on the button of the program you require. Its window will appear on top of your desktop.

The Taskbar showing two program buttons

46

Opening and saving files

In Windows 95, the dialog boxes for opening and saving files are different from those in Windows 3.1; but they work in a similar way.

For example, the picture shows a *Save As* dialog box. Type in a name for your file in the *File name* box. Select the type of file you want it stored as in the *Save as type* box. To choose the directory you are going to save your file in, open the *Save in* list, click the disk drive you require, and then double-click on the folder you want to save your file in. When you have done this, click the *Save* button.

A Windows 95 Save As dialog box

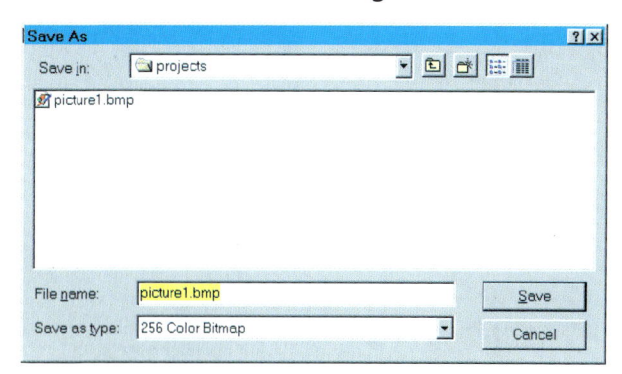

Programs and icons

Many of the applications used in this book are included in Windows 95. Some, such as Character Map and Cardfile, are exactly the same as in Windows 3.1.

Write is replaced by an application called WordPad. The WordPad window includes a Toolbar which allows you to perform certain tasks quickly, like changing type styles and cutting and pasting text.

This is the WordPad icon.

Paintbrush is replaced by Paint. Its window is quite similar and has a Toolbox and Palette that enable you to draw pictures.

This is the Paint icon.

The Display dialog box has four sections. Appearance contains a sample window display for changing your colour scheme (see pages 6 and 7). The Background section includes Desktop and Wallpaper (see pages 8 and 9, 18 and 19). Screensaver allows you to alter the screen savers on your computer (see pages 10 and 11).

The Display dialog box

Click on these labels to open a new folder.

Personalizing

You can still use Control Panel to personalize your display with pictures, patterns and colours. Click the *Start* button and select *Settings*. In the menu that appears click on Control Panel. The icon you need is the Display program shown here.

Not included

The Recorder and Object Packager applications don't appear in Windows 95. This means that you will be unable to tackle the projects in which these applications are required.

THE END

47

Index

The names of Windows applications appear in **bold** text.

active window, 30
address book, 32-33
Appearance, 47
applications
   closing, 5, 46
   opening, 4, 46
Arial, 35

.BMP files, 17, 19
background colour, 16
badges, 26-27
Brush tool, 21

.CRD files, 32
canvas, 16
Cardfile, 32-33, 36-37, 40-41, 47
cartoons, 44-45
Circle tool, 29
Character Map, 34-35, 47
characters, 34
Circle tool, 29
clip-art, 30-31, 44-45
codes, 35
Color, 6-7,
Color Eraser, 18
Color Palette, 7
colour schemes, 6-7
columns, 15
control-menu box, 4
Control Panel, 6-7, 8-9, 10-11, 18-19, 37, 47
Curve Line tool, 29
Custom Colors, 7

decoding, 35
Desktop, 8-9, 10-11, 18-19, 47
desktop, 4, 8-9
   patterns, 8-9
   saving, 9
   directories, 5

disk drives, 12, 39
Display, 47
display, 6-7

equipment, 3
Eraser tool, 17, 28, 29

File Manager, 5, 39
floppy disk, 3, 39
floppy disk drive, 12, 39
Flying Windows, 10
font, 14, 34, 35
foreground colour, 16

greetings cards, 20-21

hard disk drive, 12, 39
hidden messages, 38-39
highlight, 13

icons, 4, 5
inactive window, 30
index card, 32-33, 36, 37, 40, 41
   adding cards, 32
   editing cards, 33
interactive story, 40-41

letterhead, 13, 14
lettering, 20, 24, 25
Linesize box, 16
logo, 22-23, 27

macros, 42-45
   pausing, 45
   playback, 43, 45
   recording, 42, 45
   saving, 43
   speed, 43
   stopping, 43
Marquee, 11
Maximize button, 4, 5
Menu, 4
Menu bar, 4
Microsoft, 3
Microsoft Sound Driver, 40

Minimize button, 4, 5
mouse mats, 28-29
Mystify, 10-11

newsletter, 15
notepaper, 13

Object Packager, 36-37, 38-39, 40-41, 47
on line, 12
outlined shapes, 20
outlined text, 24

Paint, 47
Paintbrush, 16-17, 18-19, 20-21, 22-23, 24-25, 26-27, 28-29, 30-31, 32-33, 38-39, 40-41, 42-43, 44-45, 47
   lettering, 20
   printing files, 17
   saving files, 17
Palette, 16
passwords, 11
personal cards, 23
Pick tool, 23
printers, 3, 12
program groups, 4
Program Manager, 4

quiz games, 36-37

.REC files 43
Recorder, 42-45, 47
Rectangle tool, 28, 29
Roller tool; 28
ruler, 15

scaling, 29
Scissor tool, 22
screen savers, 10-11, 47
   delay, 10
   passwords, 11
   setup, 11
scroll bars, 4, 16, 20
shortcut keys, 44-45

Shrink & Grow, 27, 31
sizing
   canvas, 16
Sound, 37

Start button, 46
stencilling, 25
stencils, 24-25
stickers, 30-31

Taskbar, 46
text,
   columns, 15
   fonts, 14
   highlight, 13
   justified, 15
   size, 14
   styles, 14
Text tool, 20, 24
tile, 19
Title bar, 4
Toolbox, 16, 20

.WAV files, 37
.WRI files, 12
Wallpaper, 47
wallpaper, 18-19, 47
   choosing, 18
   customizing, 18
   designing, 18
   saving, 19
Wordpad, 47
Windows software, 3
Windows 95, 3, 46-47
window, 4-5
   active/inactive, 30
   resizing, 5, 30
   minimizing, 5
   maximizing, 5
Wordpad, 47
Write, 12-15, 22, 35, 36, 38-39, 47
   printing files, 12
   saving files, 12

Zoom In, 21
Zoom Out, 21

Box shots, photo of Microsoft hardware product and screen shots used with permission from Microsoft Corporation. Microsoft and Microsoft Windows are registered trademarks of Microsoft Corporation in the US and other countries.

First published in 1996 by Usborne Publishing Ltd, Usborne House, 83-85 Saffron Hill London EC1N 8RT, England.
Copyright © 1996 Usborne Publishing Ltd.

The name Usborne and the device are trade marks of Usborne Publishing Ltd.
All rights reserved. No part of this publication may be reproduced, stored in a retrieval system or transmitted in any form or by any means, electronic, mechanical, photocopying, recording or otherwise, without the prior permission of the publisher.
Printed in Spain